THIS BOOK
BELONGS TO

- - - - - - - - - - - - - - - - -
- - - - - - - - - - - - - - -

SELBY
SURFS

SELBY SURFS

DUNCAN BALL

with illustrations by Allan Stomann

Angus&Robertson
An imprint of HarperCollins*Publishers*

Angus&Robertson
An imprint of HarperCollins*Publishers*, Australia

First published in Australia in 1999
This edition published in 2008
by HarperCollins*Publishers* Australia Pty Limited
ABN 36 009 913 517
www.harpercollins.com.au

HarperCollins*Publishers*
25 Ryde Road, Pymble, Sydney, NSW 2073, Australia
31 View Road, Glenfield, Auckland 10, New Zealand
1–A, Hamilton House, Connaught Place, New Delhi – 110 001, India
77–85 Fulham Palace Road, London W6 8JB, United Kingdom
2 Bloor Street East, 20th floor, Toronto, Ontario M4W 1A8, Canada
10 East 53rd Street, New York NY 10022, USA

National Library of Australia Cataloguing-in-Publication data:

Ball, Duncan, 1941– .
  Selby surfs.
  ISBN 978 0 2072 0003 8 (pbk.).
  1. Dogs – Juvenile fiction. I. Stomann, Allan. II. Title.
A823.3

Cover and internal design by Matt Stanton, adapted from a design by Christa Edmonds
Cover and interal illustrations by Allan Stomann
Typeset in 14/18 Bembo by HarperCollins Design Studio
Printed and bound in Australia by Griffin Press
60gsm Bulky Paperback used by HarperCollins*Publishers* is a natural, recyclable
product made from wood grown in a combination of sustainable plantation and
regrowth forests. The manufacturing processes conform to the environmental
regulations in Tasmania, the place of manufacture.

11 10 9   09 10 11

For Callum

AUTHOR'S NOTE

Selby is not my dog. I don't own a dog. He lives in a country town which he calls 'Bogusville' with people who he calls 'Dr and Mrs Trifle'. He made these names up. He also made up the name 'Selby' so that nobody could track him down and tell the world that he knows how to talk. I don't even know his real name myself.

A while ago when he rang me to tell me about another one of his adventures I couldn't stand it any longer. 'Selby, please tell me your real name and where you really live,' I said. He was ready for this.

'Sorry,' he said, 'but I make it a rule not to tell anyone.'

'But I'm not just anyone,' I pleaded. 'I'm your biographer.'

'My what?'

'I write the stories about you. I promise I won't tell anyone. Don't you trust me?'

Selby was quiet for a moment. 'You might talk in your sleep. Someone could hear.'

'I never talk in my sleep,' I said.

'How do you know if you talk in your sleep if you're asleep when you're doing it? You could babble away all night long, for all you know.'

He had me there.

'Now do you want to hear about the time I went surfing?' he asked.

'Surfing? But you don't even know how to swim!'

'I know,' he said. 'That's what made it exciting.'

And that's how this book began.

Duncan Ball

CONTENTS

BIG INNINGS

Here are some more stories about your very own favourite talking, reading, writing — and even surfing — dog. Me! Of course I didn't actually write the stories. I told them to Duncan Ball and he did the writing. He did okay but why does he have to make everything funny? Would he think it was funny if he almost drowned? Or if a horse ran away with *him*? I doubt it.

Anyway, some really good things happened to me too. If this was a cricket match this would be my **big innings**. And here we are at the beginning of my big innings.

Happy reading!

 Selby

SELBY SURFS

'Oh, I'd love to go surfing,' Selby thought as he and the Trifles watched the International Surf-Racing Championship on TV. 'If it's this much fun to watch it must be a grillian times better to actually do it! There's just a couple of teeny tiny minor things keeping me from being a champion surfer: one, I'm a dog and two, I can't swim! Every dog except me knows how to swim as soon as they're born. It's not fair! I must have missed out on the swimming gene.'

'Look at that huge wave!' Mrs Trifle exclaimed as she handed Dr Trifle a slice of watermelon. 'It's humungous!'

'*Humungous*?' Dr Trifle said, slurping his slice.

'Very very big,' Mrs Trifle explained. 'It's bigger than all the other waves.'

'That's what they call the Colossal Curler,' Dr Trifle said. 'It happens when one wave is going faster than the others. It keeps catching them up and sucking them in like a big watery vacuum cleaner getting bigger and bigger. They're the reason that they hold the Surf-Racing Championship at Point Vertical. You see, this is surf-racing, not just surfing. Whoever goes the fastest without falling off their board wins.'

Selby watched as the surfers, one by one, dived under the approaching wave.

'Why aren't they getting up to ride it?' Mrs Trifle asked. 'Isn't it big enough?'

'I think it's too big,' Dr Trifle said.

'Yikes!' Selby thought. 'He's right! That thing's as big as a building and as fast as a freight train! Only a dare-devil would try to ride it!'

Sure enough, almost all the surfers took one look and dived under it, letting it roar by over their heads. But as the wave built up, adding more and more waves to its huge bulk, one lone surfer appeared at its top, his hair streaming backwards, his jaw thrust forward.

'*I can't believe it!*' the TV announcer cried. '*It's*

Cool Jules! The man is mad! But if he can ride this monster he'll be the champion for sure!'

The camera moved closer showing the towering wave thundering towards the beach.

'Oh, no!' Selby thought. 'The wave is starting to break! He'll be ripped to pieces!'

The crest of the wave curled gently over and the surfer disappeared.

'*He's in the pipe!'* the announcer yelled. '*If he gets out of there standing up he'll set a speed record!'*

Suddenly the wave crashed down with the roar of a jumbo jet and a great foaming mass swept up the beach.

'Where's Cool Jules?!' Selby thought as lifeguards dived into the swirling wash. 'Nothing but a fish could survive a dump like that!'

Dr and Mrs Trifle munched their watermelon furiously like a couple of harmonica players in a hurry.

'He's got to be dead,' Dr Trifle said, spitting seeds everywhere as he spoke.

A moment later a lifeguard saw something in the water and leapt in and grabbed it, pulling its limp form onto the beach. The stunned surfer struggled to his feet clasping what was left of his broken surfboard as a man with a microphone dashed to his side.

'What happened, Cool?' the man asked.

'I–I dunno, mate,' Cool Jules replied.

'What was going through your mind when you were there in the middle of the wave?'

'Well, I was like … like here I am, man. But like I do this cutback off the lip and then there's water all over the place and I'm upside down and … like before when I'm out there and I see the Curler barrelling up I'm like, "Hey! I'm outta here!" and like when I'm in the tube I'm like, "Oh, you beaudy" and I'm slewcin' —'

'Slewcin'?'

'Oh, mate! Like I'm rippin' along, spankin' the spray and it's really filthy but it's like, "What am I, mate?" You with me? I'm not thinkin', I'm just in there and it's on and like, man, then next thing I know — cowabunga!'

'Cowabunga?'

'Yeah like I'm takin' a foam nap and I'm not coming up till Christmas — ya got me?'

'Well, yes, thank you,' the announcer said. 'I hope your next ride is a bit better.'

'Gotta get me another board, mate,' replied Cool Jules. Then turning to the crowd, he asked, 'Can anybody spare a malibu?'

'Goodness me,' Mrs Trifle sighed. 'Or cowabunga, as this Jules fellow would say. He may not be great at explaining things but he certainly has guts.'

For the next hour Selby and the Trifles watched as, one after the other, the surfers tried to ride the Colossal Curlers but failed. Finally, with no one able to ride the big waves, the Surf-Racing Championship was postponed till the next day.

'The problem is the boards,' Selby thought. 'They're not made for monster waves. I'll bet Dr Trifle could come up with a perfect Colossal Curler board if he wanted to.'

'You know,' Mrs Trifle said to Dr Trifle, 'I think the problem is the surfboards. I'll bet you could invent a better one.'

'She took the words right out of my brain,' Selby thought.

'Me? Surfboards?' Dr Trifle said. 'I hardly know what one looks like.'

'So what? I think that the best inventors are people who don't know about the things they try to invent.'

'Really?'

'Yes. People who know too much never invent anything because they can always see reasons why something won't work. Ignorant people like yourself — nothing personal, dear — just go ahead and invent and sometimes their inventions work even when there's no reason why they should.'

'I love the way Mrs Trifle's mind works,' Selby thought.

'Hmmm,' Dr Trifle hmmmed, 'I'll have to think about that. Surfboards, double hmmm. I think this calls for some serious pacing.'

Dr Trifle sliced off another slice of watermelon and then started walking faster and faster around the room as he ate it.

'I still can't think of anything,' he said. 'The pacing isn't working.'

'How about just throwing out some words?' Mrs Trifle asked.

'Okay. Surfboard. Surfboard. Surf … board. Board. Wooden board. Board games. Board shorts. Bored out of my brain. Let's try surf. I can't think of anything that goes with surf.'

'Surf-vival?' Mrs Trifle laughed.

'Very funny,' Dr Trifle said seriously. 'How about water?'

'Well there's waterlily, water biscuit, waterhole, watercolour,' Mrs Trifle said, 'waterproof, water spaniel.'

'It's still not working,' Dr Trifle said, eating another piece of watermelon.

'Watermelon,' Mrs Trifle said. 'There's another water word.'

Dr Trifle looked down at his watermelon slice.

'That's it!' he cried.

'What is?'

'Of course! What do you get from watermelon?'

'Something scrummy to eat,' Mrs Trifle said.

'And seeds! Watermelon seeds. That is the answer to the Colossal Curler! The surfboards shouldn't be long and thin, they should be short and wide like watermelon seeds.'

'Are you sure?'

'It's suddenly crystal clear. What happens when you pinch a watermelon seed?'

'It goes *pahtoooooong*! and shoots across the room. When my sister, Jetty, and I were kids, I once shot one right up her nose,' Mrs Trifle giggled. 'That was so good.'

'And that's just what a surfboard should do when a huge wave comes crashing down on it. It shouldn't go flipping around up in the air, it should shoot straight out in front of the wave at a zillion kilometres an hour. *Pahtoooooong!*'

'How can a surfer stand on a board that's doing a zillion kilometres an hour?'

'Fuzzy straps.'

'Fuzzy straps?'

'You know, that stuff that sticks to itself. They'll be all over the top of the board. All the surfer has to do is put his feet where he wants to and then whack a couple of straps around his ankles and Bob's his uncle. Hmmm, I wonder if I can make one in time for tomorrow's championships.'

Selby watched as Dr Trifle worked well into the night on his melonboard: shaping pieces of styrofoam, spraying them with smelly plastics, and then doing lots and lots of sanding.

'The man is a genius,' Selby thought as he nodded off to sleep. 'He could invent anything.'

Long before sunrise, Dr and Mrs Trifle lifted the half-sleeping Selby into the car and began the long drive to Point Vertical on the Sunburn Coast. They arrived just in time for the last day of the championship.

'I can't believe how rough it is!' Selby thought as Colossal Curlers came roaring in every few minutes. 'How can anyone surf in this?!'

The boat was ready to take the surfers out around the point to the calm water beyond the surf when Dr Trifle ran up with his melonboard.

'Wait!' he cried. 'Cool Jules! I want to show you my new surfboard.'

'It looks dumb, man,' Cool said. 'Like a watermelon seed. You a surfboard designer?'

'Well, yes. This one's specifically designed for Colossal Curlers.'

'Man, I can't talk. Got this surf gig, you know?'

'I'll come out in the boat and explain, okay?'

'Sure, man.'

The Trifles and Selby piled into the boat which roared off around the point. Dr Trifle spoke about his board. Cool and the other surfers laughed and talked about it. Selby climbed up on the board to get his paws out of the water in the bottom of the boat and lay down.

Finally the boat stopped beyond the surf and all the surfers except Jules jumped in the water.

'I don't want to like hurt your feelings, man,' he said. 'But that thing's like uncool and I'm Cool Jules, know what I mean?'

'If you use that other board in surf like this,' Dr Trifle warned, 'it'll be smashed to bits. You could drown. Aren't you afraid of that?'

'Hey, man, shhhh,' Cool said. 'Not so loud. What are all those dinkuses on the board?'

'Straps,' Dr Trifle said. 'Wrap them around your ankles so you won't fall off.'

'Straps are for sissies, man. I don't do straps.'

'Oh, go ahead, Cool,' Dr Trifle said. 'Give it a go. Just once. You could win.'

'I don't know, man.'

'I wish they'd stop arguing,' Selby thought as he watched the waves forming on the other side of the boat. 'I don't like it out here, I want to get back to dry land. If a big wave comes along, I'm history. It's okay for the Trifles because they have life vests.'

Cool stared at the melonboard.

'Okay, I'll give it a go. Off the board, dog,' he said, grabbing the melonboard and jumping over the side. 'There's serious surfing to do.'

Suddenly Selby felt his world spinning like a top. He was flying through the air and then there was a great splash and he was drenched to the skin.

'Where am I? What's happening?' he thought. 'Oh, no, that fuzzy stuff that sticks to itself also sticks to other fuzzy things — namely me! I'm stuck to the straps! Get me back in the boat!'

'Cowabunga!' Mrs Trifle exclaimed without even thinking. 'Selby's stuck to the board! We've got to pull him off, quick!'

Dr and Mrs Trifle reached out and grabbed Selby by the paws while Cool Jules held the board. Then, just as they were pulling in different directions, Selby saw something coming from the other side of the boat.

'Shivers!' he thought. 'Here comes a Colossal Curler.'

'We've got to get out of here!' the man driving the boat cried. 'Sit down everyone!'

With this, the boat roared forward, pulling the Trifles loose from Selby.

'Stop!' Mrs Trifle yelled. 'I've got to rescue our dog!'

'If we don't get out of the way of that wave,' the driver called back, 'we'll all have to be rescued!'

Selby watched as the Curler picked up one wave and then another, growing all the time.

'Hey! Get offa my board, you stupid dog!' Cool yelled, still trying to prise Selby loose. 'I've gotta catch this wave!'

But all of a sudden it was too late. The huge wave lifted the board skyward and then crested. Cool Jules crouched down on top of Selby before getting to his feet.

'I said, get off!' Cool shouted again, pushing Selby with his foot.

Ahead of them the other terrified surfers, seeing the growing wave bearing down, dived under the water.

'I can't believe this!' Selby screamed in his brain. 'It's my worst nightmare come true! If this bozo chucks me off, I'm a goner. Oh, woe woe woe.'

Selby watched as the wave grew higher and higher, its crest spitting a line of white foam into the air.

'Oh, you beaudy!' Cool cried. 'This is the wave of a lifetime! If I can only get this dog offa here I could win this thing!'

Cool reached down and grabbed Selby's front paws, pulling them away from the board but Selby's hind paws stayed stuck, leaving him standing up in front of Jules.

'Oh, well,' Cool said. 'I guess we're in this together.'

On and on they tore as the mammoth wave swept along over the reef, churning up sand, seaweed and rocks as it went.

'Yeeeeeeeeehaaaaaaaaaaaaaawwwwwww!' Cool screamed as the wave leaned over. 'She's barrelling up! Cowabunga! I'm in the tube!'

'This guy's nuts!' Selby thought. 'In a second, the whole thing's going to crash down on us. If the melonboard shoots out in front the way it's supposed to, I might survive but Cool could be history! I've got to talk to him.'

Selby turned his head and looked up at Cool Jules.

'Now listen to me, Cool, and listen good,' he said. 'Crouch down and grab my waist.'

'P-P-Pardon me?' the shocked surfer stammered. 'Did you ... speak?'

'Forget about that. Just hang on to me or you'll drown, okay?'

'But you're a dog. You can't talk.'

'Hey, am I talking or what?' Selby said. 'Grab me, you ninny! It's your only chance!'

Cool got down on his knees behind Selby and clutched him around the waist just as the wave came crashing down on them. Selby held his breath, suspended in space, and waited.

'The watermelon seed action isn't working!' Selby thought. 'But Dr Trifle just *has* to be right!'

Just then he felt the water pressing down on top and then up from under them squeezing like a thumb and finger squeezing a watermelon seed. Suddenly there was a huge *pahtooooooong!* and the board shot forward, skipping over the waves in front of them.

'Look at that!' someone screamed. 'A dog riding a surfboard!'

Up onto the beach they went and the judges watched, dumbfounded, as Selby grabbed the trophy before they skidded to a stop. In a second the television crew rushed over to them.

'That was the most fantastic thing I've ever seen!' the television interviewer cried. 'You've won the championship, Cool! And you did it the hard way with the dog on your board!'

'No, you don't understand, man,' Cool said. 'That dog is like ...'

'Oh, no,' Selby thought. 'I'm happy to be alive and I'm glad that the melonboard worked but now Cool Jules is going to give away my secret.'

'Like what, Cool?' the interviewer asked.

'Filthy.'

'Filthy?'

'Awesome. Like we're in there, man, and he's like, "Grab me! Grab me!" And I'm like, "Whoa, man, what's happening?" and the board like shoots out *pahtooooooong*! man, like that.'

'That surf really knocks you around, doesn't it champ?'

'B–But like the dog —'

'I know, he's a real champion too. Thank you Cool but we have to go to an ad break. Congratulations. This is Rod Morrison at surfside. And now back to the studio.'

As the cameras turned away, Mrs Trifle ran up and took Selby out of Cool Jules' arms.

'Is he okay?' she asked.

'The grommet? Sure. He's fantastic! I mean I'm here talking and like I could be — know what I mean?🐾 — still out there havin' a surf nap. But like it's not like that cuz he's like, "Hang onto me!" and like ... weird man. Double weird. Hey, thanks for the board. It was really filthy, mate.'

'He's not a bad guy, Cool,' Selby thought as Cool Jules walked away shaking his head. 'I'm just glad he's a better surfer than he is a talker.'

🐾 *Paw note: This is a question-comma. You can use it in the middle of sentences.*   S

SELBY STUCK

'Look how sharp this is!' Dr Trifle said, stabbing the dagger he'd just made into his workbench.

'Goodness! That *is* sharp!' Mrs Trifle said, pouring some new Dry-Mouth Dog Flakes into Selby's bowl. 'Here, try some of these, Selby. You seem to like Dry-Mouth Dog Biscuits so you should *love* these.'

'Only I *hate* Dry-Mouth Dog Biscuits,' Selby thought as he stared at the bowl. 'So I know I'll *detest* these.'

'And now watch this,' Dr Trifle said, pointing the dagger towards himself.

'Gulp. What's he doing?' Selby thought as he looked up from sniffing the Dog Flakes.

'Please don't joke,' Mrs Trifle said. 'It makes me nervous when you pretend like that.'

'So who's pretending?' Dr Trifle said. 'I've had enough. Goodbye, oh terrible world. Goodbye. Goodbye.'

Selby watched in horror as Dr Trifle stretched his arm out ready to stab himself.

'Don't do it!' Mrs Trifle screamed. 'I'll make your favourite lunch! Stop!'

A sad look came to Dr Trifle's face and then he plunged the knife into his chest before collapsing backwards to the floor. A spot of blood spread outward from the dagger until it covered the front of his shirt.

'What have you done?!' Mrs Trifle screamed. 'Don't move! I'll ring an ambulance!'

Selby took a quick breath, nearly inhaling a Dry-Mouth Dog Flake.

'He's killed himself!' Selby squealed to himself. 'Dr Trifle just stabbed himself in the chest with that dagger! I can't believe it! This is awful!'

Suddenly Dr Trifle opened his eyes and let out a big laugh.

'Oh, you,' Mrs Trifle sighed. 'You gave me a terrible fright. Don't ever play that sort of game again, do you hear?'

'Sorry but it wasn't a game. I was just testing my newly-invented trick dagger. I had to know if it looks real. I could tell from your face that it did.'

'So who needs trick daggers?'

'We do. It will be perfect for *You Know Who*, the murder mystery play that we're going to act in with the Bogusville Stagestompers.' 🐾

'But there's blood all over your shirt,' Mrs Trifle said. 'How did you do that?'

'It's only red ink; the oldest trick in the trick dagger book,' Dr Trifle said, pushing the point of the dagger with his finger. 'The blade slides up into the handle. It only looks like it's gone into the victim. When the blade goes up it squeezes a sponge that's filled with ink and the ink comes squirting out. Don't worry, it's the sort of ink that washes out easily.'

'But I saw that dagger stick into your workbench.'

'Ahah! That's the second oldest trick in the trick dagger book. Do you see this little knob on the handle? If it's in this position, the blade

🐾 *Paw note: If you want to read a story about me actually acting with the Stagestompers, read 'The Enchanted Dog' in the book* Selby's Secret. **S**

20

slides in. If it's in this position, it locks and can't slide into the handle.'

'That's marvellous,' Mrs Trifle said. 'Which character gets stabbed in the play? I haven't even got round to reading the script yet.'

'The murderer does. At the end of the play, the detective — that's me — discovers who the murderer is. The murderer then grabs the murder weapon — the dagger — and tries to kill the detective.'

'That sounds awful.'

'It's a comedy, really. It's all just fun. Anyway, the detective manages to grab the murderer's arm and turn the dagger around and, well, the baddie gets it.'

'So who plays the part of the murderer?'

'Well, that's the thing,' Dr Trifle said. '*You Know Who* is one of those plays that has a surprise ending.'

'A surprise ending?'

'Yes, there's a different murderer every night.'

'How is that possible?'

'Towards the end of the play, the detective stops the show and asks the audience who they want the murderer to be. They vote by putting up their hands. Let's say they choose Postie Paterson. Then the detective points to Postie and says, "I know you're the one who committed this terrible crime. You gave yourself away when you said such and such." And then I list all the other clues. The murder weapon is there, sticking into the kitchen table. Postie then grabs the dagger and has a go at me.'

'I see,' Mrs Trifle said. 'So you have to remember lots of different clues because the audience might choose Postie one night and Melanie Mildew the next night.'

'Or Mrs Poppycock,' Dr Trifle said. 'Which is you.'

'Since I'm the mayor they'll probably choose me every night just for fun. Please make sure you grease the blade of that dagger well. If it doesn't slide up into the handle Bogusville will be looking for a new mayor.'

'Don't you worry about a thing. Hmmm, the handle's coming apart,' Dr Trifle said. He took the two sides of the handle off. Then, grabbing a can of *Glu-It-All* glue from the shelf over his workbench, he glued them back together.

'There, now it's perfect,' he said.

★ ★ ★

For the next two weeks, whenever they had time, Dr and Mrs Trifle paced around the house practising their lines. And so they did right up to the day the play opened.

'It had to be you, Mrs Poppycock,' Dr Trifle said, pointing his finger at Mrs Trifle. 'All the evidence points to you. You gave yourself away when you said that you'd taken the four o'clock train to Adelaide. There's a three-twenty train and a four-fifteen train but no four o'clock train. There's never been a four o'clock train to Adelaide.'

'Okay, you've found me out, Inspector Wembley,' Mrs Trifle said. 'But she deserved everything she got. She never should have said all those terrible things about me. And now it's your turn!'

With this, Mrs Trifle grabbed the dagger and she and Dr Trifle wrestled with it until it plunged into Mrs Trifle's chest.

'Okay, okay,' Mrs Trifle said. 'I think we're ready for tonight's performance. But before that, I've got a council meeting. Want to come along?'

'I'd love to,' Dr Trifle said. 'If I keep rehearsing I'll only make myself more nervous.'

'That Dr Trifle is so clever,' Selby thought when the Trifles were safely out of the house.

Selby crept into Dr Trifle's workroom and had a good old play with the dagger. He stabbed it into the workbench and then flipped the knob to the other position.

'Goodbye cruel world,' he said, holding the dagger over his chest. 'I've eaten my last Dry-Mouth Dog Flake.'

With this he stabbed himself in the chest.

'Ouch! That hurt!' he said, inspecting the blade. 'It didn't slide into the handle as easily as it should have. I think it needs some grease.'

Selby grabbed the can of *Grease-It-All* grease from the shelf and dropped some drops of it on the knife blade before sliding it in and out again.

'That slides more easily,' he said. 'Now no one can get hurt. Oh, I wish I could see the play tonight.'

Selby was in luck. After the council meeting Dr and Mrs Trifle picked him up, took him to the theatre and left him backstage with a bowl of Dry-Mouth Dog Flakes.

'I'm so nervous,' Mrs Trifle said before the curtain went up. 'I'm afraid I'll forget my lines. And I'm a little frightened of that dagger too.'

'It's fine,' Dr Trifle said. 'You worry too much.'

Selby watched the play quietly from backstage. 'This is great!' he thought. 'I wonder who the audience is going to choose to be the murderer tonight!'

At the end of the play, Dr Trifle gathered all the suspects together and then turned to the audience.

'Now it's your turn,' he said. 'Who do you think was the murderer? I'll bet that *you know who*.'

'Oh, this is sooooo tense!' Selby thought as he took another mouthful of Dog Flakes. 'I can't stand it!'

Suddenly the audience chanted loudly 'Mrs Poppycock. Mrs Poppycock. Mrs Tri-fle! Mrs Tri-fle!'

'And Mrs Poppycock it is!' cried Dr Trifle. 'You guessed it.'

'Okay, you've found me out, Inspector Wembley,' Mrs Trifle said. 'But she deserved everything she got. She never should have said all those terrible things about me.'

Mrs Trifle pulled the dagger from the table.

'And now it's your turn, Inspector!' Mrs Trifle screamed.

Dr and Mrs Trifle wrestled for the dagger.

'This is sooooo scary!' Selby squealed in his brain. 'It's like the real thing! Their acting is sooooooooo good. They're like proper actors.'

All four hands gripped the dagger and slowly it turned away from Dr Trifle and poised above Mrs Trifle's chest.

'Oh, no! Now she's about to be stabbed,' Selby thought. 'It's only pretend. It's only pretend. It's only pretend.'

Just then, a terrible thought started making its way through Selby's brain.

'Uh-oh! What if I put *Glu-It-All* glue in the dagger instead of *Grease-It-All* grease?! What if I took the wrong can without noticing? I was in a hurry and the names are almost the same. They were right together on the shelf! What if the blade won't slide in? No, I couldn't have made such a stupid mistake. But maybe I did. No, I couldn't have. But what if I did?

Couldn't have. Could have. Couldn't have. Could have.'

The thought went round and round in Selby's brain like a toy train on a track to nowhere. Finally it burst out the other end.

'I can't take the chance!' he squealed to himself. 'If anything happens to Mrs Trifle it will be all my fault! It'll be on my conscience forever! I have to stop them and there's only one way to do it! Who cares if everyone (gulp) finds out my secret?!'

Selby leapt onto the stage and jumped between the Trifles, pushing them apart. He was about to cry 'Stop! Don't do it!' in plain English when suddenly a Dry-Mouth Dog Flake caught in his windpipe. He began coughing and wheezing, trying to get the words out. In a minute he was clutching his throat and his whole face turned bright red.

The audience burst into laughter at the sight of the coughing dog.

'The dog did it!' someone screamed.

For a moment, Dr Trifle and the cast just stood there wondering what to do. Finally it was too much and the Trifles, along with the

rest of the cast, started laughing along with the audience. Then someone lowered the curtain.

'This is a disaster!' Mrs Trifle said to Dr Trifle.

'I know. What do you suppose got into Selby?'

'He thought we were really fighting, poor dear,' Mrs Trifle said. 'Dogs get upset when they think their owners are fighting.'

When the curtain went up again the actors bowed to wild applause.

'They loved it!' Mrs Trifle whispered. 'It was a success after all!'

'We certainly gave them a surprise ending,' Dr Trifle said. As he held Selby up to cheers and even wilder applause, he accidentally dropped the dagger.

'My goodness!' Mrs Trifle gasped, as she saw the dagger stick firmly into the floor where it had fallen. 'The blade didn't slide! It looks like it was almost a surprise ending for me! That silly invention of yours would have killed me if it hadn't been for Selby! It would have stuck right into me!'

'And luckily for me,' Selby thought, suddenly happy that he'd held the Trifles apart. 'I was stuck too — only I was stuck for words.'

SELBY'S LAMINGTON DRIVE

Selby worked frantically all day and through the night making hundreds of lamingtons. First he baked dozens of sponge cakes. Then he sliced them into little squares and put them in the fridge. When they were cool he dipped them in chocolate and rolled them in dried coconut.

'Wow! These are fantabulous! They're just like real lammos,' Selby thought as he gobbled one and then another. 'What am I talking about? They *are* real lammos,' he added, scoffing down a third one. 'Lammo bammo! Yummo bummo! These are delicious!'

Selby was just finishing his baking when he caught sight of himself in a mirror.

'Is that me?' he wondered. 'I can hardly recognise myself. I'm covered from head to toe in chocolate and coconut! I look like a big lamington with ears and a tail! I'd better get cleaned up before Aunt Jetty catches me. How did I ever get myself into this mess?!'

Getting into the mess had been simple: it all began the day he overheard Mrs Trifle telling Dr Trifle about a letter she was waiting for that never arrived. Someone had put the wrong address on it.

'The problem is that no one ever remembers the name of our street,' she explained. 'Bunya-Bunya Crescent is such a strange name. It's hard to spell and easy to forget. People are always writing things like Bunions Crescent or Bumpkin Crescent or even Bungle Bungle Crescent. Who decided to name the street Bunya-Bunya Crescent anyway?'

'You can blame my great-grandfather, Terfle Trifle, for that,' Dr Trifle said. 'He built this very house back when the street was just a dirt road and there weren't any other houses on it. Then he named the street after that beautiful old Bunya-Bunya tree down the road. He loved Bunya-Bunyas.'

'It's a pity he didn't like oaks or wattles or bluegums instead,' Mrs Trifle said. 'We could be living on Oak Crescent or Wattle Drive or Bluegum Street. They would be so much easier for people to spell — and for people to remember. I've got an idea: why don't we rename the street?'

'But what would we name it? Bogusville already has a Wattle Street and an Oak Avenue and even a Bluegum Lane,' Dr Trifle said. 'So we couldn't use those names. Besides, street names are street names — you can't change them.'

'Of course you can.'

'Are you sure?'

'I am the mayor of Bogusville, remember,' Mrs Trifle said. 'I ought to know.'

'So how would we do it?'

'Simple, all we'd have to do is choose a name and get our neighbours to sign a petition saying that they all agree. Then give it to the council for approval.'

'That sounds easy.'

'You have to fill out a form, of course,' Mrs Trifle added.

'I hate council forms,' Dr Trifle said. 'They're always so complicated. They use so many big words that I have to look up in the dictionary.'

'We've just changed all the council's forms. They're now written very simply and clearly. They're absolutely idiot-proof.'

'You mean even I could fill one out?'

'Of course you could, dear.'

'Okay, then let's do it,' Dr Trifle said, getting excited. 'What's a good name for our street? Think of one.'

'Oh, I forgot to say that there's a street renaming fee of one hundred dollars,' Mrs Trifle said.

'*One hundred dollars?* Why so much?' asked Dr Trifle, as he suddenly thought of all the things he could buy if he had a hundred dollars.

'Someone has to pay for the new street signs,' Mrs Trifle explained. 'And if we're the ones who want to change the name, we're the ones who should pay for it. It's only fair.'

'Bunya-Bunya Crescent is beginning to sound good again,' Dr Trifle said. 'Let's just leave it the way it is.'

Selby had been lying on the floor listening to all this but it was later that day, when the Trifles were away, that he got his idea — an idea so brilliant that it took his breath away.

'I've just thought of the perfect street name!' he gasped. 'Why not call it *Trifle Terrace* after the Trifles?! They're such dear sweet wonderful people. It would be lovely to name the street after them. Besides, Trifle is easier to remember than Bunya-Bunya. I am so clever. Sometimes I scare myself.'

Selby scratched his head and looked out the window.

'Of course I'll have to get the name changed without the Trifles knowing. They'd be too embarrassed to change it to their own name themselves. But I think they'll love it once it's done.'

Selby jumped to his feet and began pacing the floor.

'Hmmm. How will I get the neighbours to agree to this? They may not be so keen on naming the street after the Trifles. Hey, now! Hold the show! I'll tell everyone that we're *not* naming it after the Trifles. We're naming it after the first person to live in the street — Terfle Trifle. And because *Terfle Trifle Terrace* is too long I'll tell them that we decided to shorten it to Trifle Terrace. Oh, Selby, you are a brilliant dog! Now how will I come up with the hundred smackeroos?'

Selby paced faster and faster, his mind racing like a jet engine.

'I know!' he cried, trying to snap his toes the way people snap their fingers when they have a brilliant idea. 'I'll use the oldest money-raising trick there is — I'll sell lamingtons! I'll have a lamington drive!'

And so it was that Selby's brilliant idea started him off on a road to total disaster. But I won't spoil the story by jumping ahead . . .

The next thing Selby did was ring the council offices, put on his best Dr Trifle voice, and ask to be sent a copy of *Street Renaming Form Number 142b/66*. The day it arrived, Selby waited in a bush near the mailbox. When Postie

Paterson dropped off the day's mail, Selby quickly grabbed the envelope with the form in it and hid it so the Trifles wouldn't see it.

Then came the Easter long weekend when he knew that the Trifles would be away at the Sunburn Coast delivering another melonboard for Cool Jules to test.

'Now all I have to do is make sure that Aunt Jetty doesn't catch me cooking when she pops in to put food in my bowl,' Selby thought.

Selby cooked all through the night until he was completely exhausted and so covered in chocolate and coconut that he looked like a big lamington with ears and a tail. All of which brings us back to the beginning of this story.

'So far, so good,' he thought as he stepped out of the shower looking like a new dog but feeling like he'd been up all night long — which, of course, he had. 'I've got the lammos. Now for the lamington drive.'

Selby crept out of the house just before sunrise and set up a folding table at the end of the street. On it was a huge box with two hundred lamingtons in it, a piece of paper, and a sign that said:

LET'S RENAME THIS STREET TRIFLE TERRACE
AFTER TERFLE TRIFLE: THE FIRST PERSON TO LIVE IN THE STREET.
SIGN THE PETITION AND BUY SOME LAMMOS FOR ONLY
50 CENTS EACH TO PAY FOR THE NEW STREET SIGNS.

Then Selby sneaked back home before anyone saw him.

Within two hours the lamingtons had all been sold and everyone on Bunya-Bunya Crescent had signed the petition. Selby, now barely able to keep his eyes open, dragged himself out again, grabbed the box — which had exactly one hundred dollars in it.

'Now to fill in the *Street Renaming Form*,' he said as he sat down at the Trifles' desk. 'Let's see now. "*Old name of street.*" "*New name of street.*" "*How was money raised?*" Mrs Trifle was right — this form is so simple that it's idiot-proof. But I can barely keep my eyes open. Oh, well, here goes.'

Selby filled in the blanks on the form and put it and the money into an envelope before staggering down the street to post it.

When the Trifles returned that afternoon, Selby was sound asleep.

Two weeks later Selby had almost forgotten about the street name when he heard the sound of hammering outside. Mrs Trifle came racing in.

'You'll never guess what's happened?!' she cried. 'It's so exciting! We don't live on Bunya-Bunya Crescent anymore!'

'Goodness! Where do we live?' Dr Trifle said, looking out the window to see if the street looked familiar. 'I don't remember moving house — do you?'

'No, silly, someone must have got the same idea we had: they've renamed the street. It's no longer called Bunya-Bunya Crescent.'

Selby got up and stretched. He could feel the warmth of his achievement flow through him like a cup of hot cocoa. The good deed that he'd wanted to do for the Trifles for so long was now finally done — and no one would ever guess that he was the one who did it.

'So what street *do* we live in now?' Dr Trifle asked, squinting to read the street sign in the distance. 'I can't quite make out the name.'

'I'll give you a hint,' Mrs Trifle said. 'It's a kind of food.'

'Food?' said Dr Trifle.

'Food?' thought Selby as he raced to the window. 'What is she talking about? Oh, of course! How silly of me! A *trifle* is a kind of dessert. She thinks that Trifle Terrace was named after the food and not after her and Dr Trifle. Isn't that a laugh?'

Selby rubbed his eyes and looked across the street. The old Bunya–Bunya Crescent sign now lay on the ground and the new one, with bright blue letters, stood on the pole above it. It said:

LAMINGTON DRIVE

'Lamington Drive?!' Selby screamed in his brain. 'It's supposed to say Trifle Terrace! 🐾 not Lamington Drive! Someone at the council must have made a mistake!'

'I guess everyone else in the street was having trouble with the name Bunya–Bunya Crescent,' Mrs Trifle said, 'so they changed it. Do you like the name?'

'I like it,' Dr Trifle said, 'but it'll take some getting used to.'

> 🐾 *Paw note: This is my other cool invention — the exclamation-comma. You can use this one in the middle of a sentence too!*
>
> S

'Yes,' Mrs Trifle said, 'and I'll get hungry every time I see the sign.'

'Every time *I* see the sign,' Selby thought, 'I'll get sick to my stomach! I just realised what happened: I must have made a mistake when I filled out the *Street Renaming Form*. I put the bit about *how the money was raised?* in the space for the *new name of the street!* It's all my fault! Those new forms may have been *idiot-proof* but they weren't quite *Selby-proof*.'

SADDLE-SORE
SELBY

'Saddle up, girls!' called Mrs Martingale, the owner of the Slippery Saddles Riding School. 'Lunch is over. Time for another ride.'

From where Selby was hiding in the hayloft he heard a loud groan.

'I'll have none of that!' Mrs Martingale said sharply. 'Don't be such wimps! You're just a little saddle-sore, that's all. Nobody ever died from being saddle-sore. You'll never learn to ride properly if you don't practise.'

Selby peeked out as the girls climbed back on their horses.

'What about these horses?' Prunella asked, pointing to two horses still in their stalls.

'Shouldn't we be riding them too? They haven't had any exercise all day.'

'Well, that's very thoughtful of you, Prune,' Mrs Martingale said. 'But Sleepytime Sal is very old and very tired. She can only really be ridden by a small child. If one of you rode her, you'd be lagging behind all the time and it would be too much for her.'

'How about the other one?' one of the other girls asked.

'That's Mr Wiggle,' Mrs Martingale said. 'He's a very valuable showjumping horse. He's so highly strung that only an expert could ride him. He actually belongs to Somerset Stud Farm.'

'What's he doing here at the riding school?' Prunella asked.

'That's a bit of a secret, Prune,' Mrs Martingale said in a low voice. 'His owners are afraid of horse thieves. Someone tried to steal him recently and his owners are now putting security alarms in the stables and installing a big metal gate.'

'So you're looking after him while they're doing the work, is that it?'

'You're too clever for your own good, Prune. Yes, just for a day or two. No one knows he's here so you're all sworn to secrecy, okay?'

'Where's Selby?' one of the girls asked. 'Can't he come along?'

'He's probably asleep somewhere,' Mrs Martingale said. 'We must have worn him out this morning. Come along now.'

'You can say that again,' Selby thought as he watched the girls ride across the paddock and into the woods. 'I never wanted to become these girls' private pet. It's all Mrs Trifle's fault. Whenever the girls go on an outing they ask Mrs Trifle if it's okay to take me along — and it's *always* okay with her! How about me? I spent all morning running to keep up with those horses. That's not my idea of a good time.'

Selby peered over the edge of the loft and looked at the horses that had been left behind.

'I feel sorry for these two. Sleepytime Sal is okay I guess but poor Mr Wiggle,' he thought as he watched the horse move back and forth in his stall. 'He's so frisky. He'll go bonkers cooped up in there all day.'

Selby lay there watching.

'Horses. Why do girls go completely ga-ga over horses? Dogs are so much more fun. They jump on your lap and lick you. They chase sticks — well, some of them do. But I guess you can't ride a dog. Maybe it isn't the horses they like but the riding. Sitting on a horse's back. Bouncing around. Weird. Of course, I have no idea what it's like because I've never done it.'

Selby looked at the sleepy horse and then the frisky one.

'How hard can it be to ride a dopey old horse like Sleepytime Sal?' he wondered. 'Maybe I'll just have a quick ride around the ring to see what all the fuss is about.'

Selby climbed up the side of one of the stalls and pulled a saddle off a rail.

'Wake up there, Sal,' he said, putting the saddle on the sleepy horse. 'Don't panic but you're in for a treat. You're about to be ridden by a real live dog — a talking one at that. Hmmm, let's see, how does this seat belt go on? It must go around the horse's belly.'

Selby jumped into the stall, climbed under the horse and fastened the girth. He opened the door and then climbed up on a stool.

'Steady on, Sal, my gal,' he said, climbing into the saddle. 'That's a good girl. Okay now, go! Move it out there. Oooooooo. This feels all rocky and funny. I think I need a seat belt for myself.'

The horse walked slowly out of the stall, then into the riding ring and out the open gate and into the paddock.

'Oooops, I meant to close that,' Selby thought. 'Oh, well. Come on, this is getting boring. How about a little action, Sal?' Selby said, as the horse broke into a trot. 'That's more like it. Okay, now turn right! Come on, Sal, I said, turn! Struth! Where are the handlebars on this thing? Uh-oh, I forgot to put those steering string things on her. But I know what to do,' Selby said, grabbing a pawful of mane, 'I'll steer her with this. I saw someone do it in a movie on TV.'

The horse was going faster and broke into a canter as it went through another open gate and down the hill.

'Stop it, Sal! Stop! Whoa! What are you doing? Not that way! If the girls see me I'm a done dog! They'll know I'm not an ordinary non-talking non-horse-riding dog! Turn around! Go back! About face! You're supposed to be sleepy and slow and you're as fast as a fire engine!'

Selby stopped pulling on the mane and clung to the saddle with all paws as the horse shot down through a gully, across a stream and up the side of a hill.

'I can't stop her and I can't jump off because she's going too fast!' Selby thought as he saw the girls' horses on the track ahead.

'Oh, nooooooo!' he cried. 'The seat belt is loosening up! I'm going down!'

Selby and the saddle slid around under the horse with Selby still clinging to it. Then, as he flashed past the girls, he heard Mrs Martingale cry, 'Mr Wiggle is loose! There's movement at the station! The colt from Somerset has got away! After him, girls!'

'Mr Wiggle?' Selby thought as he clung for dear life. 'But I thought you were a girl.' Selby turned his head around to look backwards towards the girls. 'Gulp. You're no girl, that's for sure. Oh, no! I'm riding a champion showjumper!'

Down through the valley Mr Wiggle tore with Selby clinging underneath and a thundering herd of screaming girls riding close behind.

'There's something clinging to Mr Wiggle's belly!' Prunella yelled.

'Oh, no, they've seen me!' Selby thought. 'I can't let go now or they'll trample me and if I let them catch up they'll know the *clinging thing* is me!'

Selby thought about what would happen when they caught up to him and found out his secret. Sure, the girls would be delighted. They'd take him back to the stables and they'd all sit around and have a nice chat and plenty of pats. He'd tell them that being a dog was like being a person only better. And then they'd take him home and tell Dr and Mrs Trifle. They, too, would be happy at first but then it would start: 'Selby, would you mind scooping the leaves off the swimming pool while we're out today?' Or: 'Selby, could you ring all these people and tell them about the council meeting tonight?' Or: 'Selby, would you mind cleaning the toilet?'

'No! No! No! I can't stand it!' Selby thought. 'I don't want to be found out!'

Just then one of the girls screamed, 'Look out!' And in that instant Mr Wiggle leapt high in the air over a row of dense bushes. Then he landed on the other side and came to a stop. In a second Mrs Martingale and the girls came around the bushes and surrounded him.

'The lump on Mr Wiggle's belly is gone!' Prunella exclaimed.

'And look at this,' Mrs Martingale laughed. 'Some nitwit tried to steal Mr Wiggle but didn't tighten the girth properly. I suspect the horse-napper got a nasty surprise!'

'He certainly did,' Selby thought when he crept out of the bushes and limped back towards the stables. 'And I don't think this nitwit is likely to do it again!'

THE S-FILES

'The Trifles have been captured by aliens!' Selby screamed as he looked at the burnt circle in the grass. 'This is where the spaceship took off! What do I do? Who do I call?!'

It all began the night before when Dr Trifle was working on a new invention in his workroom and Mrs Trifle was settling down to watch their favourite TV alien adventure program.

'Oh, I'm so glad the Trifles like that show because I absolutely adore it and I can watch too!' Selby thought as Dr Trifle put another bolt into his invention. 'The stories are so spooky. And those special investigators are great! He's so handsome and she is so beautiful.'

'It's show time,' Mrs Trifle sang out from the next room.

Dr Trifle stopped work and went into the loungeroom. Selby darted after him.

'Oh, boy!' Selby thought as he curled up in his favourite spot next to the lounge. 'I can feel the tingles creeping up my spine already and the show hasn't even started!'

The episode was about an inventor who had suddenly disappeared. Soon the two special investigators arrived on the scene.

'I think I know what's happened here,' the man said. 'He's been abducted by aliens.'

'Very unlikely,' the woman said. 'Why do you think it was aliens?'

'This invention was obviously something the aliens didn't want him to be working on.'

'It looks like a can opener to me.'

'How can it be a can opener? It's as big as a fridge.'

'It's for big cans.'

'His notes say that he was working on an invention that would unlock the secrets of the universe. Look, the invention has the initials S-O-T-U written on the side.'

'SOTU? Is that a word?'

'It stands for *Secrets Of The Universe*.'

'But one of the neighbours saw a group of very short people with wild hair come to the door the night he disappeared,' the man said. 'How do you explain that?'

'Short? Wild hair? Girl Guides. Probably Girl Guides selling chocolates to collect money for a camp.'

'But then the neighbours heard the man screaming his head off.'

'So maybe he didn't like chocolates,' the woman said. 'I don't like chocolates either. Give me a chocolate and I'll scream my head off too. Let's get out of here.'

'Not so fast. How do you explain that circle of burnt grass?' the man asked.

'How do *you* explain it?'

'That's obviously where the spaceship took off.'

'I think the Girl Guides had a campfire and a big singsong. They like to do those things. If you want I'll sing you some campfire songs.'

'But the man has disappeared! There's got to be a reason for it.'

'Okay so he was abducted by Girl Guides and force-fed chocolates. Then they made him listen to campfire songs before they took him away. They'll bring him back. Let's get out of here.'

'This is sooooo frustrating!' Selby thought. 'She never believes a word he says! It drives me nuts! But I can't stop watching the program. It's great!'

Selby and the Trifles watched in silence as the two investigators dashed from one crime scene to the next, fighting off evil agents, and nearly being killed a dozen times.

'What was that all about?' Dr Trifle said. 'I was completely lost by the end of it.'

'So was I,' Mrs Trifle said. 'But I can't wait to see what happens next week.'

'Oh, well, back to my invention,' Dr Trifle said, heading for his workroom.

'Another invention to unlock the secrets of the universe?' Mrs Trifle said with a chuckle.

'Shhhh,' the doctor said. 'The aliens will hear you.'

'How can he make jokes like that?!' Selby thought. 'I still have shivers from that show.'

★ ★ ★

That night aliens came and took Selby away. Well they didn't really but that's what he dreamt. He also had nightmares about a huge white worm that was taking over Bogusville.

The next morning Selby awoke to an eerie calm.

'Why is it so quiet around here?' he thought. 'Usually the Trifles are having breakfast. Or Dr Trifle is banging away in his workroom.'

Selby trotted into the kitchen and began eating the Dry-Mouth Dog Biscuits in his bowl.

'It's as creepy as a graveyard in here,' he thought as he looked around the house. 'They've gone out. But their car's still in the driveway. They never go anywhere without their car. This is really weird.'

Selby looked out the front door and saw something strange in the field across the street. He dashed over and found a big round circle of burnt grass. Next to it lay Dr Trifle's new invention.

'I can't believe it!' Selby cried as he read the initials S-O-T-U painted on the side of the

invention. 'The doctor wasn't kidding! He was onto something! S–O–T–U must stand for *Secrets Of The Universe*. He was about to unlock them! The Trifles have been captured by aliens! Help! This is where the spaceship took off! What do I do? Who do I call?!'

Selby ran to the phone and dialled 000.

'What is the nature of your emergency?' the voice said.

'Pardon?' Selby said.

'Police? Fire? Ambulance?'

'No, none of those,' Selby said. 'I don't know if you can help me.'

'We can help you with any emergency, sir, just tell us what it is.'

'Well I think my owners — I mean, the people I live with — have been abducted by aliens.'

'Domestic or extraterrestrial?'

'I beg your pardon?'

'Were they aliens from somewhere on the earth or from outer space?'

'Outer space, I think,' Selby said. 'They took off in a spaceship.'

'Putting you through,' the voice said.

The next voice Selby heard said, 'You have reached the Extraterrestrial Unit of the Department of Alien Enquiries. If you wish to speak to someone about buying a copy of our *Guide to the Identification of Extraterrestrial Aliens*, press 1. If you wish to know where the most recent extraterrestrial sightings have taken place, press 2. If you wish to hear the sound of an extraterrestrial spaceship taking off, press 3. If you are going to attend the Annual Extraterrestrial Conference and require a hotel booking, press 4 — please have your credit card ready —'

'I don't want any of that!' Selby squealed. 'This is stupid!'

'If you are an extraterrestrial alien ringing, press 5 —'

'No, I'm *not* an extraterrestrial alien!' Selby screamed. 'Will you hurry up?'

'— If you or someone you know has been abducted by extraterrestrials, press 6.'

'Finally!' Selby sighed, pressing the 6 button on the telephone.

'You have now reached the Extraterrestrial Unit of the Department of Alien Enquiries'

Extraterrestrial Aliens' Abduction Unit, or the E-U-D-A-E-E-A-A-U which is pronounced eooda-eeyau. If the person abducted was you, press 1 —'

'Oh, this is stupid!' Selby cried. 'Can't I talk to a real person?'

'— if the abductee or abductees, if there were more than one — is or are strangers, press 2 —'

'Well, no, they're not strangers.'

'— If they were relatives, press 3 —'

'No, they're not relatives, for heaven's sake. What does it matter? They're gone and aliens have abducted them, okay? They'll be passing Venus by now.'

'If they were friends, press 4.'

'That's it!' Selby said, pressing 4 on the telephone.

'Extraterrestrial Unit of the Department of Alien Enquiries' Extraterrestrial Aliens' Abduction Unit, Friends' Abductions Team, Fred speaking. How may I help you?'

'Fred, you're just the man I want. You see these people I live with —'

'They're not relatives, are they? If they are, I'll have to put you in touch with our relatives' team.'

'No! No, Fred, hold the show. They're definitely friends. Good friends —'

'And you are?'

'Selby. I mean Selwyn —'

'Let's stay with Selby, shall we, Mr Selby? No made up names, please.'

'Okay, Fred, now listen carefully. Dr and Mrs Trifle of Bunya–Bunya Crescent in Bogusville — sorry, it's now called Lamington Drive —'

'Lamington Drive? I once organised a lamington drive —'

'Fred! They've been abducted by aliens!'

'They have? When?'

'Last night. There's a round burnt circle in the grass and everything!'

'This sounds serious. We'll be right there. In the meantime, don't answer the phone and don't open the door to strangers,' Fred said. And then, just before he put the phone down Selby heard Fred say, 'Grab your gun, Effy, this could be a real one.'

An hour later a helicopter landed in the field and two investigators — a man and a woman —

got out and studied the burnt circle and Dr Trifle's invention. Selby crept out of the house and got close enough to hear what they were saying.

'I don't know, Fred,' the woman said. 'I think it's another hoax. It'll be the seventh one this week.'

'Why do you think it's a hoax, Effy?'

'You know that aliens program you always watch on TV?'

'Yes?'

'Someone told me the plot of last night's episode this morning. It was about an inventor who disappears. There's a burnt circle of grass from the spaceship taking off. The inventor's invention that has S-O-T-U painted on it is left behind on the ground. It's just like this. Someone saw last night's episode and they're pulling our leg.'

'Legs, Effy. You're so negative.'

'Me? Negative? We've already had fifty hoaxes this month. We haven't had a *real* alien abduction yet. Of course I'm negative.'

'Well I have a theory about this one.'

'What is it?'

'It was *aliens* who watched that TV program last night.'

'You mean that's where they got the idea to abduct an inventor — from TV?'

'Exactly.'

'I hadn't thought of that, Fred. Have you run a check on the Trifles?'

'They're real people all right, Effy. Well they were till the aliens got to them.'

'How about this Mr Selby?'

'Well, that's a different matter.'

'What do you mean?'

'Let's leave Mr Selby out of this.'

'Come on, Fred. Is there a Mr Selby?'

'Yes ... only he's a dog, okay? He's the Trifles' pet dog.'

'And you're saying this *isn't* a hoax? Stop pretending that it's not. You do this all the time.'

'Okay, okay, so it's a hoax. You don't get it, do you?'

'Get what?'

'Do you want us to go back to our old jobs, Effy?'

'You mean, at the Lost and Found, Fred?'

'Exactly.'

'Of course not. I hated working there. If I ever see another lost umbrella, I'll scream.'

'If we don't find something that's really supernatural soon, they're going to get rid of the whole department and we'll be back working at the Lost and Found.'

'This is serious. Okay, let's start investigating. What do we do?'

'Just the usual. We take some pictures, we make some notes, and we take the invention back to the office. Maybe they'll believe us this time.'

'This makes me sick!' Selby thought. 'The Trifles have been whisked away by aliens and these doofuses are worried about keeping their jobs! I'm going to give them a piece of my mind. A talking dog — make that a *screaming* dog — should be supernatural enough for them!'

Just as the agents were lifting Dr Trifle's invention into the helicopter, Selby stepped up and was about to say, 'Hey! What do you think you're doing?!'

Then, suddenly, Selby heard a voice behind him say, 'Hey! What do you think you're doing?!'

Selby wheeled around to see Dr and Mrs Trifle standing there.

'Where do you think you're going with my husband's invention?' Mrs Trifle demanded.

The agents turned around.

'You mean . . . this is yours?' the man said.

'Yes, of course it is. Who are you?' Dr Trifle asked.

'Well I'm Fred and this is Effy. We work for . . .'

'The Lost and Found,' Effy said. 'Don't we, Fred?'

'Well if we don't, we soon will, Effy,' Fred said.

'The Lost and Found?' Dr Trifle said. 'And you fly around in a helicopter?'

'Yes, it's easier to find things that way.'

'Oh, I see,' Dr Trifle laughed. 'I'm terribly sorry. No, it wasn't lost. I was just trying to get it to work when my wife said we should go for a walk instead. So I just left it here.'

'I see,' Fred said as the two of them climbed into their helicopter. 'But what exactly does your invention do?'

'It's a lawn-mower that runs on solar power. This lens focuses the sun's rays and, instead of *cutting* the grass, it *burns* it off.'

'That's brilliant!' Effy said. 'But what does S-O-T-U stand for?'

'Scorcher Of The Undergrowth,' Dr Trifle replied. 'Only it's not working.'

'What's wrong?'

'I don't know but it keeps running around in circles. See the mark it made?'

'Goodness me,' Selby thought as he headed back towards the house. 'That machine isn't the only thing that's been running around in circles — so have I.'

ALIENS!

❧

As I was walking by the sea
A spaceship landed next to me
And out stepped twenty freaky creatures
With wobbly legs and knobbly features.

Then as I turned to run away
They zapped me with a blue-green ray
And I was frozen to the spot
Yes, I was well and truly caught!

A purple blob with giant nose
And sixteen legs in two long rows
Came slithering right up to me
And opened fourteen eyes to see.

She was a girl, this much I know:
Her ears were tied with a big pink bow.
I tried my best but couldn't shout
She'd scared my living daylights out!

Some awful thoughts ran through my head
In thirty seconds I'd be dead
She'd cut me up from head to toe
Just to see what made me go.

If I survived, for all I knew
I'd land in some galactic zoo!
An earthling dog for all to see
Locked up for all eternity.

Then suddenly her arm reached out
And wrapped itself around my snout
My mind was in a dreadful muddle
Oooops! She was giving me a cuddle!

And patting me! How could this be?
And winking all her eyes at me!
Suddenly I was enraptured
So what if I had just been captured.

Perhaps they'd treat me like a king
I'd wave a paw and have them bring
Whatever would best suit my mood:
A prezzie or some yummy food.

What's this? They jumped back in their craft
And closed the windows fore and aft
Then in the blinking of an eye
They blasted off into the sky.

In a moment, I connected:
They'd left me there – I'd been rejected!
Alas, it was quite plain to see
They didn't want a dog like me.

'Come back!' I cried. I yelled abuse
Alas it wasn't any use.
I walked along beside the sea
And thought, 'Oh woe, oh woe is me.'

Selby

SELBY'S
SET-UP

'Did you know that they're going to be filming a real movie with real movie stars in my library?' Camilla Bonzer, the librarian at Bogusville Primary School, asked.

'Yes, we know,' Mrs Trifle said.

'And guess what?'

'What?'

Camilla sat down on the lounge next to Selby and began patting him. 'Dino diSwarve, the most gorgeous actor in the whole universe, is the star and he's going to be in my library and I'm going to get to meet him! Isn't that exciting?!'

'He is quite good looking,' Mrs Trifle said. 'But I'm not sure he's much of an actor.'

'Oh, who cares about that,' Camilla said. 'I could just look at him forever. He's so dishy! Do you know what the film is about?'

'Yes, and I know the script for the film was written by an old friend of ours, Gary Gaggs.'

'Not *the* Gary Gaggs? the comedian?' she said. 'His jokes cheered me up when I was so upset last year, remember? 🐾 Are you sure he wrote it? This movie is a romance not a comedy.'

'It's a romantic comedy,' Mrs Trifle said. 'It's called *A Binding Friendship* and it's about a librarian and someone who falls in love with her. That's all I know.'

'Well I know more than that because I read about it in the *Dino diSwarve Fan Magazine*.'

'You read the *Dino diSwarve Fan Magazine*?'

'Of course, he's sooooo handsome! I have posters of him all around my house and I'm the president of the Bogusville Dino diSwarve Fan Club, too. Let me tell you about the story. Dino plays this really shy young man who lives at

🐾 *Paw note: She's right. Read about it in the story 'Books, Bombs and Book Week' in the book* Selby Spacedog. S

71

home with his mother and doesn't have a job or friends or anything.'

'But he usually plays rough, tough jokey guys.'

'Not in this movie. He goes to the library all the time and borrows science-fiction books. Of course this is supposed to be a normal library and not a school library like mine but never mind. Anyway, the librarian falls in love with him. She wears all these glam clothes and everything. But he doesn't notice her because he's so shy he never really looks at her. She's played by what's-her-name, the actress with the big smile and all the teeth.'

'I can't remember her name either,' Mrs Trifle said.

'Anyway, one day old tooth-face slips a romance book in with his sci-fi books when he checks them out of the library. It's one of those Kiss'n'Tell books or Party Pashers books that the girls all read.'

'Don't tell me,' Mrs Trifle said. 'He discovers the book, reads it and falls in love with the librarian.'

'No,' Camilla said. 'This is the interesting thing. The movie has two endings.'

'How can a movie have two endings?'

'It just does. In one of them he notices her and falls in love and they end up together. In the other one, she falls in love with this other guy who's been after her forever.'

'So you can decide which ending you like the best, is that it?' Mrs Trifle asked.

'That's it. I've got to go now before the shops close because I'm buying a new dress. I'm meeting Dino tomorrow.'

'So that he will fall in love with you and take you away to Hollywood with him and live happily ever after?' Mrs Trifle said with a laugh.

Camilla gave her an icy stare and stopped patting Selby.

'It could happen,' she said. 'It *could* and I think it will.'

'Do you really?'

'Frankly, yes, I do.'

'Poor Camilla,' Mrs Trifle said to Dr Trifle after the librarian had gone. 'I think she lives in a fantasy world.'

'What do you mean?'

'She really thinks that Dino diSwarve, a world famous, super-rich, and quite-good-looking-if-you-ask-me movie star is going to fall in love with her.'

'It could happen,' Dr Trifle said, looking up from his newspaper.

'How could it?'

'Well if he got to know her he'd realise that she's a very interesting person. Then he might fall in love and even marry her.'

'Oh, heavens. Movie stars don't fall in love with teacher-librarians. Everyone knows that. Everyone except Camilla. I do worry about her.'

'Mrs Trifle's right,' Selby thought. 'Camilla's just going to make herself unhappy by hoping that Dino will fall in love with her. I wish she'd be more realistic. Oh, well, there's nothing I can do. Anyway, I wonder if I can sneak into the library and watch the filming tomorrow. That sounds like good fun.'

The next day was Saturday and there were no schoolchildren at Camilla's library when Selby arrived but the street outside was in total chaos. There were trucks and more trucks filled with movie cameras, lights, props and other equipment. And there were people running in every direction, talking to each other through their headsets. Sneaking into the library was the easiest thing that Selby had ever done.

'An elephant could walk in here and nobody would notice,' Selby thought as he looked around at the people inside. 'Look! There's Gary Gaggs! And there's Camilla! Oh, no! She bought a really expensive-looking floral dress just to meet Dino in. Poor Camilla.'

In the bright lights in front of the camera, the director talked to the actor.

'That's him!' Selby squealed in his brain. 'It's the real Dino diSwarve! I can't believe I'm actually looking at him. He certainly is a lot shorter than he is in his films.'

'Okay,' called the director. 'Quiet on the set everyone! Roll 'em! Let's see if we can get it right this time. Come in, Bonnie.'

Selby watched as the actress who was playing the librarian came out of the office and walked up to Dino.

'Bonnie Blake?' Selby thought. 'It's her! It's Bonnie Blake! I absolutely adore Bonnie Blake! Well, I adore her but I don't think I'd want to marry her,' he added. 🐾

'Hello, Ron,' Bonnie said, smiling at Dino and batting her eyelashes. 'How are you today?'

Dino looked at her and gave a broad smile.

'Hi, Janey, baby,' he said. 'I'm great. How about you?'

'Cut!' the director yelled. 'No, no, Dino. You're not supposed to look at her. Look down at the ground. And you're supposed to mumble, "I'm — I'm sorry is the library closing or something".'

'But that's stupid,' Dino said.

'That's what the script says.'

'So what? Who cares about the stupid script?'

'Your character is very shy,' the director said. 'He wouldn't say, "Hi, Janey, baby".'

'Well I'm not going to play him shy. I always play a jokey kind of tough guy. That's the real me. I want to be me.'

🐾 *Paw note: For more about me and Bonnie, read the story 'Selby Lovestruck' in the book* Selby Snowbound. S

'But that's not what this movie is about,' the director said. 'He's got to be shy or the story doesn't work. I hired you to play a shy guy.'

'Who's kidding who? You hired me because I've got a million fans out there and they love to go to movies if I'm in them. They don't want to see me playing a wimp.'

Bonnie Blake glared at him.

'You can't do it, can you?' she said.

'What do you mean?'

'You can only play yourself because you don't know how to act.'

'Whoa! Of course I can act.'

'No, you can't.'

'Can!'

'Can't!'

'What would you know about acting?' Dino said. 'You're nothing but a soapie star. I'm a big time movie star.'

'At least I went to acting school. They picked you because of your looks and that's all.'

'Stop!' the director yelled. 'I want to talk to you individually in my trailer. Bonnie, come with me, please.'

Dino just sat there as the director and the crew left the library. Selby hid behind a row of books, watching. Suddenly Camilla appeared from behind another row of books and walked up to the actor.

'Oh, no!' Selby thought. 'She's going to talk to him. She should stay right away from him.'

'Who are you?' Dino snapped.

'I-I'm Camilla Bonzer,' Camilla said with a trembling voice. 'I'm the librarian here.'

'So what? It's Saturday. Go home.'

'I-I-I know, Mr diSwarve. B-But I'm your greatest fan.'

'Yeah, right.'

'I am. I've got posters of you all around my house.'

'So what? Lots of people have them. Could you just leave me alone ... please?'

'This is sooooo embarrassing!' Selby thought. 'Why doesn't she just go away?'

'I'm also the president of the Dino diSwarve Fan Club.'

'You're pulling my leg.'

'It's true,' Camilla said weakly. 'I wouldn't lie to you, Dino.'

Selby could see tears forming in Camilla's eyes.

'Like the Australian Dino diSwarve Fan Club?'

'Well no. The *Bogusville* Dino diSwarve Fan Club.'

Dino laughed. 'What, all six of you?' he said.

'Actually, I'm the only one in the club,' Camilla admitted.

'Camilla! Don't do this to yourself!' Selby thought. 'He's treating you like dirt! Just stay away from him!'

'I heard the argument you had with Bonnie Blake,' Camilla said. 'And I think I have a book you might like to read. Here. It's very popular with the kids. Of course I can't give it to you because it's the library's copy. But you can borrow it.'

Dino took the book in his hands.

'What is this? *Even You Can Act*. Are you kidding? This is an insult!'

'No, no, no, Camilla,' Selby thought, covering his eyes with one paw and shaking his head. 'You're making it worse and worse. Forget the book. Just go away.'

'I–I know this sounds silly giving a book on acting to a super-famous actor,' Camilla said. 'But I think it's really very good. There are a lot of acting tips in it that they don't even teach in acting school. It says so on the back cover. Look. Remember, no matter how much we know about something we can always learn more.'

Dino leapt to his feet and threw the book on the floor. 'Get out of here!' he screamed.

'But I love you,' Camilla pleaded, the tears now streaming down her face. 'I want to go away with you and live in Hollywood. You'll like me when you get to know me. I want to marry you, Dino.'

'Rack off you … you … you *librarian* you!'

Camilla cried even harder and ran from the library. Selby followed her down the street to Bogusville Park. There she sat on a park bench, weeping.

'Poor, poor Camilla,' Selby thought. He climbed up next to her and lay down. 'That guy was so cruel to her! I should have bitten his leg off!'

'Selby,' Camilla sighed. 'You sweetie. If I didn't know better, I'd think you came here to cheer me up.'

'I did, Camilla,' Selby thought. 'Believe me, I did.'

Camilla patted him.

'Remember when I chucked a wobbly in the library?' she said. 'You were there then, too. It really helped. Remember Gary Gaggs' corny jokes? He's so funny.'

'That's the kind of guy for you, Camilla,' Selby thought. 'Not some dumb, short, movie mega-star who can't act for beans.'

'Oh, Selby Selby Selby, what am I going to do? Why does life have to be so sad?'

'Life doesn't always have to be sad, Camilla,' Selby thought. 'Oh, how I wish I could just talk to her and tell her that she's the one who's making herself sad. I've got it!' Selby thought again. 'Maybe I could get Camilla and Gary Gaggs together. They'd be perfect for each other.'

With this, Selby jumped down and ran back to the school. He ducked into an empty classroom and found some paper and a pencil.

And this is what Selby wrote:

I have always liked you. Please come away and talk
to me. I will wait for you at the park at the end of
the street.
Your friend,
Camilla
PS: Please tear this note up and never mention it to
anyone.

'Now all I have to do is give it to Gary,' Selby thought.

The filming had started again in the library. This time Dino was acting very shy and using the words from the script as Gary Gaggs and a hundred others watched quietly.

It was a stealthy Selby who sneaked up to slip the note in Gary's hand.

'Bonnie, darling, we're going to get that hair of yours moving, okay?' the director called. 'Okay, keep the scene going you two. Hey, somebody turn on the wind machine.'

With Gary's hand hanging down to his side, Selby sneaked up from behind and slipped the note between his fingers. He then ducked back into the crowd, unnoticed. But just as the note touched Gary's hand, the wind came up and blew it away. It tumbled over and over on the ground . . .

Gary looked down at his hand to see what had touched it and then raced forward, snatching the note from the floor. He read it in silence before turning to see if he could catch a glimpse of the mysterious messenger.

'What's he going to do?' Selby thought. 'Come on, Gary! Go to the park!'

Gary read the note again. After the third time he tore it up and hurried off down the street.

'Yesssssssssssssss!' Selby hissed as he ran after Gary. 'It worked!'

Gary found Camilla sitting on the bench.

'Camilla,' he said.

'Gary?' she said back.

'I don't know quite how to put this.'

'What is it, Gary?'

'Well I-I . . . '

'Yes, Gary?'

'What a lovely dress you're wearing.'

'Do you like it?'

'Yes and I like you too,' Gary said very quickly.

'Oh, Gary,' Camilla gushed.

'When I wrote the script for the film I was thinking of you.'

'You were? I was the librarian? I was Bonnie Blake?'

'Yes, and guess who the man who really wanted a girlfriend was? Me. I can get up and tell jokes to hundreds of people but I'm really very shy. I was too shy to tell you how much I liked you. That's what made me think of the story for the film,' Gary explained. 'And now ... well, here we are.'

'Yes, we are, Gary,' Camilla said, reaching out and taking his hands in hers. 'You're such a lovely person. And you have such a wonderful sense of humour. Could you tell me a joke?'

'Sure. Do you know how scientists weigh whales?'

'No, how do they, Gary?'

'They take them to a whale weigh station,' Gary said with a great laugh. And then he put his thumbs in his armpits and strutted around like a chicken saying, 'Woo! Woo! Woo! Sorry, but I like to do that when I tell a joke.'

'I love it!' Camilla said. 'Tell me another one.'

'Did you hear the one about the bloke who put egg whites in his gun? He wanted to make a boom-meringue. Get it? Woo! Woo! Woo!' Gary said. 'Get it?'

'Boom-meringue?' Camilla said. 'Oh, I get it.'

'I don't get it,' Selby thought. 'Oh, I know, you make meringues with egg whites! That's great!'

'How about the two ants who ran away and secretly got married? They were ant-elopes. Woo! Woo! Woo! Then there was this train that liked to eat all the time. It was a *chew chew* train. Woo! Woo! Woo!'

'This is fantabulous!' Selby thought as he trotted off towards home. 'Gary's jokes are wonderful! He's the perfect guy for Camilla. I'm sure they'll make each other very happy.'

And so it was that Gary Gaggs and Camilla Bonzer fell in love and had a wonderful time together.

★ ★ ★

Gary looked down at his hand to see what had touched it and then raced forward. But he was too late. The paper made its way between the legs of the camera crew and lodged in the open copy of *Even You Can Act* that lay at Dino's feet.

'Cut!' the director called. 'That's a wrap for the day. Okay, kids, you were great. Your limos will pick you up at six tomorrow morning.'

Dino picked up the book and saw the note.

'Oh, no!' Selby thought. 'He'll think it's from Camilla to him.'

Dino read the note and then tore it up, throwing the pieces on the floor.

'He's torn it up. Good,' Selby thought. 'Now to write another one and get it to Gary Gaggs. Hmmm, how will I do it?'

Selby was just searching for more paper and another pencil when he noticed Dino hurrying off down the street towards Bogusville Park.

'I can't believe it! He's going to be nasty to Camilla again!' Selby thought. 'But not if I have anything to say about it! I'll fix that useless little twerp!'

Selby raced after Dino but didn't catch up to him until the actor had reached the park bench where Camilla sat weeping.

'Camilla,' he said.

'Dino?????' she said back.

'I don't know quite how to put this.'

'What is it, Dino?'

'Well I-I . . .'

'Yes, Dino?'

'What a lovely dress you're wearing.'

'Thank you.'

'I'm really here to apologise for being so rude to you,' Dino said very quickly. 'It was unforgivable. I was just so tense because I couldn't play my part in the movie. Bonnie was right, I really didn't know how to do anything but play myself.'

'I shouldn't have said anything,' Camilla said. 'It's just that I really wanted to meet you.'

'That book saved my life,' Dino said. 'I had a look at it during our break. It's true that it was aimed at kids but some of the things it said about acting were . . . how can I say this?'

'You learned some important things, did you?'

'Exactly.'

'Well, you're forgiven, Dino,' Camilla said. 'I think we've both learned something important today. I learned that I shouldn't fall in love with mega–super–movie stars.'

'Camilla . . .?' Dino said.

'Yes, Dino?' Camilla said back.

'I think I love you.'

'You do? How is that possible?' Camilla said, taking his hand in hers.

'I don't know but that's how I feel. Would you like to come dancing with me tonight? That lovely dress would be perfect to wear to a fancy nightclub.'

'But there aren't any fancy nightclubs in Bogusville, Dino. There aren't even any un-fancy ones.'

'I have my private jet. We could fly off to the city and dance till dawn. How about it, Camilla?'

'Oh, Dino, Dino, Dino, of course I'd love to. This is my dream come true.'

For a moment Camilla and Dino stood, hand in hand looking into each other's eyes.

'Well,' Selby thought, 'this wasn't exactly how the note was supposed to work but it certainly worked. Oh, isn't it lovely (sigh) that Camilla's wish came true.'

And so it was that Dino diSwarve and Camilla Bonzer danced the night away. When the movie was finished they moved to Hollywood where Dino continued to be a mega-super-star and Camilla started a library for movie stars and filled it with books about movies and acting and actors.

Author's note: This is the way Selby told me this story. He told me both endings. When I begged him to tell me how it really ended he said, 'Take your pick.' Only when I told him that I wasn't going to put it in this book did he tell me the real ending. Believe it or not, the real ending was the one about Camilla and Dino getting together. But there was more to it.

After a while Camilla got tired of Dino and tired of living in Hollywood. She started her library but found out that actors never came in to borrow books — they were too busy going to the movies and watching TV. She left Dino and moved back to Bogusville where she and Gary Gaggs fell in love.

Well that's what Selby told me so I guess I have to believe it.

Duncan

SOOP-ADOOP-ALOO

'What? Tear down the public toilet at the sports ground?' Aunt Jetty gasped. 'You can't just ditch a dunny like that!'

'We have to,' Mrs Trifle said. 'It gets vandalised every week. The council can't afford to keep fixing it.'

Selby peered out from under the lounge as Aunt Jetty's dreadful son, Willy, and his equally dreadful brother, Billy, ran around the house looking for him.

'Where's that doggy?' Willy squealed as he tore by. 'I'm gonna get him!'

'You can't just get rid of a toilet because someone paints a rude word or two on the walls,'

Aunt Jetty said. 'Willy and Billy play footie at that field every weekend. How are they supposed to go to the loo if there's no loo to go to?'

'They can wait till they get home,' said Mrs Trifle.

'You're the mayor,' Aunt Jetty said. 'Get a council worker to paint over the graffiti every now and then.'

'It's not just graffiti. Someone is plugging up the toilet, too.'

'With what?'

'Sticks, frisbies, school uniforms, you name it.'

'Then catch them and have them arrested.'

'I'm not going to ask a police officer to hide in the loo all week hoping to catch the culprit. I'm sorry but it's going to be goodbye PCRF.'

'PC what?'

'PCRF. That's council talk. Our technical name for a public toilet is a Public Convenience Relief Facility.'

Later, when Aunt Jetty and her sons were safely out of the house, Selby crawled out from under the lounge, and Dr Trifle emerged from his workroom.

'Did I hear you say that you were going to dump the dunny at the sports ground?' Dr Trifle asked.

'I'm afraid so.'

'Well I've been doing a lot of thinking about toilets recently and it seems to me that what the world needs is an un-graffiti-able, un-plug-up-able public loo.'

'I'm sure that's true.'

'Well you may be interested to hear that I've already drawn up the plans and I was just about to make the first one.'

'What a wonderful coincidence,' Mrs Trifle said.

'That's what I love about Dr Trifle,' Selby thought. 'While other inventors are thinking about computers and space travel, he invents inventions that really matter to people. While their heads are in the clouds, his head is in the toilet. Only I'm not sure that's the right way to say it.'

Two weeks later Mrs Trifle came home to find Dr Trifle in the backyard standing next to a big square metal box taller than he was.

'Have a look at my newly invented SDP for the PCRF at the sports ground,' Dr Trifle said, flinging open the door and revealing the very strange looking toilet inside.

'Your SDP?' Mrs Trifle said with a frown.

'My Super Duper Pooper,' Dr Trifle said.

'Oh, I'm not sure about the name. Perhaps you could call it an SDL,' Mrs Trifle said. 'A Super Duper Loo. Even better, make it an SAA: a Soop-Adoop-Aloo.'

'That sounds good,' Dr Trifle said, handing Mrs Trifle a can of spray paint. 'Now step inside and write something rude on the wall.'

Mrs Trifle stepped into the loo and sprayed the words DR TRIFLE IS A — and then stopped.

'What's wrong?'

'I can't write anything rude about you dear. Besides, I don't know any rude words.'

'Oh, go ahead. You'll think of something.'

Mrs Trifle hesitated and then finished the sentence. It said:

DR TRIFLE IS A SILLY BOTTOM

'Charming,' he mumbled. 'So that's what you think of me.'

'I don't really think you're a silly bottom, dear,' Mrs Trifle said. 'In fact you're a very clever bottom.'

'Okay, watch this,' Dr Trifle said.

Suddenly there was a gurgling and a bubbling and water streamed down the inside of the walls washing Mrs Trifle's words away.

'That's fantastic!' Selby thought. 'Automatic self-cleaning toilet walls! Dr Trifle is brilliant!'

'How did you do that?' Mrs Trifle asked.

'Simple. The walls are painted with my newly invented anti-graffiti paint, Graff-Rid. The Loo-Brain does the rest.'

'The Loo-Brain?'

'That's what I call my automatic control system. When someone puts paint on the walls it knows it and sends special chemicals streaming down to wash it off.'

'But what if the vandals scratch the words in the paint?'

'Try it,' Dr Trifle said, handing Mrs Trifle a nail.

Mrs Trifle tried to scratch her name into the paint but couldn't.

'Goodness!' she exclaimed. 'This paint is very hard.'

'Graff-Rid is made with a powder of the same super hard metals as space vehicles. This paint would stop a rocket.'

'Dr Trifle has to be the smartest person in the whole world!' Selby thought. 'No one else could make a loo that would stop a rocket?!'

'This is all absolutely wonderful, dear,' Mrs Trifle said. 'But the biggest problem with the PCRF at the sports ground is that someone is plugging it up.'

'I've thought of that,' Dr Trifle said, handing Mrs Trifle an old worn out beach towel. 'Go ahead, flush this down the loo.'

Mrs Trifle threw the towel into the toilet and flushed. For a minute the water rose. Then there was a sudden series of sucking and gushing noises followed by a big gulp and a huge burping noise as the towel disappeared.

'Why that's wonderful!' Mrs Trifle exclaimed. 'But what about bigger things?'

'This big?' Dr Trifle asked, handing her a basketball.

'That's silly. A basketball can't fit down a loo.'

'Try it.'

Mrs Trifle put the basketball into the toilet

and flushed. Selby and the Trifles watched and listened as the water rose. The series of sucking and gurgling noises increased and, finally, with the basketball stuck firmly in the bottom of the toilet, there was a huge *pop*! and the ball shot out of the toilet followed by a gush of water.

'It didn't flush,' Mrs Trifle said.

'But it didn't clog up either. If something refuses to go down the hole then the pressure reverses and it pushes it out. The Loo-Brain has a mind of its own which makes this toilet unplugable. Well it's not a *mind* mind, just a little doover that ticks over when the pressure gets up to the red zone. Then the whole cycle goes into flip-flop mode and then *whammo splasho ploppo* out comes the basketball. It's a flush or fling toilet.'

'Heavens!' Mrs Trifle exclaimed, looking at the wet spots on her blouse. 'I think I've been splashed with you-know-what from the toilet!'

'It's just a jet of clean water. I keep the pressure gauge low so that no you-know-what or even what-do-you-call-'ems can come back out.'

'Well that's a relief,' Mrs Trifle said.

'Oh, and I forgot to tell you that when the system flip-flops, a vandal alarm rings. Another one goes off in the police station so the police can come running and catch the culprit.'

'You are a marvel,' Mrs Trifle said, giving her husband a big hug. 'Will your SAA be ready to put in the PCRF in time for Saturday's kiddies' footie match?'

'Absolutely.'

Sure enough, the following Saturday Selby followed Dr and Mrs Trifle down the street to the sports ground where the Soop-Adoop-Aloo had been installed earlier that morning. He hid in the bushes and watched Willy and Billy play in the weekly footie match. Afterwards, as the crowd was leaving, he saw Dr Trifle go into the loo and come out again.

'No one's tried to damage it,' he reported. 'So I guess it wasn't much of a test.'

'No one's going to try any funny business while there are so many people around,' Mrs Trifle said. 'The moment we leave, I'll bet the vandals will strike. Jetty,' she said turning to her sister, 'how about coming back to our place for lunch?'

'No, I have things to do at home,' Aunt Jetty said. 'Come along, boys.'

'No!' screamed Willy. 'I don't want to go home now! I want to stay here and play footie with Billy!'

'Me too!' Billy screamed, kicking the football over the top of a small tree. 'We can walk home later.'

'All right, boys, but be good,' Aunt Jetty said. 'And remember you've got clean clothes in your sports bags. Change out of those grubby clothes so you'll be respectable when you come home. That'll be a nice surprise for mummy.'

'Okay, Mummy,' Willy and Billy said together.

'Those monsters couldn't be good if their lives depended on it,' Selby thought. 'I'm going to stay right here and keep an eye on them.'

As soon as the adults were out of sight, Willy reached into his sports bag and got out a can of spray paint.

'Hey, Billy!' Willy said, dashing into the SAA. 'Guess what you are?!'

'That's not fair!' Billy yelled, running in after him.

'I knew it!' Selby thought as he snuck around behind the toilet. 'Willy and Billy were the culprits all along! They're the ones who have been destroying the loo.'

Selby watched from the tiny window at the back of the SAA as Willy started writing on the wall.

'*Billy is a* — He's a what?! I don't even know what that word means!' Selby thought.

'Gimme that!' Billy screamed, grabbing the can out of Willy's hands and changing the *B* in Billy to a *W* to make it Willy.

Suddenly there was a gurgle and liquid poured down the wall, washing away the words.

'What the . . . ?!' Billy said. 'It's gone! That's not fair.'

'Fair enough for you,' Selby thought.

'Watch this!' Willy said, getting a big nail out of his pocket and trying to a scratch a word on the wall. 'Hey! I can't scratch it! What's going on?!'

'I'll tell you what's going on,' Selby thought. 'Your little bird-brains are no match for Dr Trifle's brain.'

'Let's go home and watch videos,' Billy said. 'This is no fun.'

Selby watched as Willy and Billy took off their dirty footie clothes and boots. Then, just as they were going to get clean clothes out of their sports bags, Willy said, 'I know! Let's block up the pooper!'

'Let's do it!' Billy squealed.

With this he picked up Willy's football clothes and threw them in the toilet.

'No!' Willy screamed.

But it was too late. For a minute the water rose, then there was a sudden series of sucking and gushing noises, a big gulp and a huge *burp*! and Willy's clothes disappeared down the hole.

'That was so much fun!' Billy giggled.

But before he could think, Willy had flushed Billy's clothes down, too.

'You stupy stinkbottom!' Billy screamed as he threw Willy's sports bag in the loo and flushed.

Again there were gushings and suckings and gulpings and then, just before Willy's sports bag disappeared, Willy threw Billy's in too. With one loud *burp*! they were gone.

'Now look what you've done!' Billy cried, punching his brother.

'Me?!' Willy wailed as he punched Billy back. 'You started it!'

Selby's smile turned into a grin as Willy and Billy punched it out in the SAA.

'I don't think I've had so much fun in years,' Selby thought. 'If I could get this on video I'd watch it every time I wanted a good laugh.'

Finally, the fight finished with both boys in tears.

'I'll fix that stupy stinkypoo dunny!' Willy cried as he threw their one last possession — the football — into the toilet. 'This will break it!'

'Don't count on it,' Selby thought.

For a few moments there were suckings and gushings and gurglings as the water rose and fell. The football stuck fast in the bottom.

'It's too big to flush,' Selby thought. 'So now the Loo-Brain's going to fling it.'

Selby watched the needle go up and up towards the red zone, setting off the vandal alarm.

'What's that noise?!' Willy screamed, clapping his hands over his ears.

'I don't know!' Billy screamed back.

'Oh, no!' Selby thought. 'The needle is already up in the red zone but nothing's happening! The ball is just the wrong size! The Loo-Brain can't make up its mind between flushing or flinging! I'll have to turn up the pressure!'

Selby noticed a bright red tap at the back of the Soop-Adoop-Aloo. 'This must be the water pressure valve,' he thought. He opened the valve more and more and watched the arrow shoot past the red zone and to the very top of the dial. Suddenly there was a rumbling like an earthquake and then an ear-splitting *burp*! The cycle flip-flopped again and the football shot up so hard that it pounded around the inside of the dunny like a stray ping-pong ball. And following it was a geyser of liquid. Only this time it wasn't just clean water.

When Sergeant Short and Constable Long pulled up in their police car there were Willy and Billy, standing outside the SAA crying their eyes out.

'Goodness me,' Sergeant Short said. 'What have we here?'

'They appear to be Aunt Jetty's sons Willy and Billy,' Constable Long said. 'They're all wet and filthy and they seem to have misplaced their clothes. You don't suppose they were trying to damage Dr Trifle's new toilet, do you, Sergeant?'

'Well if they were,' the sergeant said. 'I'm sure they'll never try it again.'

'We won't do it again, honest!' Willy cried.

'I see,' Constable Long said. 'Well, I guess we'd better give them a lift home and tell their mother.'

'Hold on a tick. Do you smell what I smell?' Sergeant Short asked.

Constable Long stepped closer to the boys and then pulled back, quickly, holding his nose.

'If I'm not mistaken,' the constable said. 'These boys are covered in ... well in ... you-know-what.'

'Yes, and I think I smell what-do-you-call-'ems too.'

'Do you really want our nice new police car to smell like you-know-what and what-do-you-call-'ems?' the constable said.

'No, I don't think I do, Constable. Goodness me, look at the time! We'd better get back to the police station.'

Selby watched as the policemen walked back towards their car, laughing as they went.

'You have to take us home!' Willy screamed.

'You can't make us walk home in the nuddy!' Billy screamed too.

'Did you hear something?' Constable Long said.

'No, I didn't hear anything,' Sergeant Short said as they drove away.

Selby rubbed his paws together and giggled with delight as the police drove away and Willy and Billy started their embarrassing walk home.

'Thanks to Dr Trifle's invention, Willy and Billy just got the biggest surprise of their lives. And when they get home I think Aunt Jetty is going to get a nice surprise too!' Selby thought. 'Oh, joy, oh, joy. Isn't life wonderful?'

WILLY

Oh, Willy Willy Willy-woo
Forgive me for not liking you.
It isn't nice; I know it's silly,
But I don't care for you – or Billy.

Sometimes I have an awful thought,
And wonder if I would be caught
If I should reach right down your snout
And pull your insides inside out.

I'd give you a karate chop
Just to see your eyeballs pop.
And then (and this is really mean)
I'd use you as a trampoline.

Oh, Willy Willy Willy-woo
Forgive me for not liking you.
I know it isn't nice to hate
But in your case it feels just great.

PEEP-DIPPER

'I'm going to have to cancel the Farmers' Fancy Dress Charity Ball,' Mrs Trifle said.

'But why?' Dr Trifle asked. 'Bogusville needs the money that the Charity Ball raises.'

'The farmers are all very generous but we end up paying more to put the hall back in order than we get in donations.'

'Are you saying that the farmers trash the place?'

'Of course not. Not on purpose, at least. The problem is that some of them drive great distances on dirt roads and by the time they get here they're covered in dust.'

'So what does a little dust matter?'

'It all ends up on the dance floor. By the time they finish dancing the floor is so scuffed and scratched that we have to have it polished and painted again. That costs more than the money we collect. What good is a charity ball when there's no money left for charity?'

'We could ask them to change into clean clothes and shoes before they go into the hall,' Dr Trifle suggested.

'That's ridiculous. We'd have to provide dressing rooms. The next thing you're going to say is that we should dip them.'

'Dip them?'

'The way farmers push sheep and cattle into water that's filled with chemicals. That would get all the dirt and dust off them,' Mrs Trifle said. 'Don't worry, I'm just kidding.'

'Kidding? No, I think you're absolutely right.'

'Oh, don't be silly. Can you imagine all those people letting someone chuck them into a tankful of water before they were allowed into the hall? They simply wouldn't have it.'

'I'm not so sure. Just let me think about this for a while,' Dr Trifle said. 'Hmmm. I think I still have some of the bits and pieces from that old car wash.'

'It wouldn't work because they'd all be

dripping wet and that wouldn't be good for the dance floor either,' Mrs Trifle said. 'Besides, the Charity Ball is only a week away. I think we'll have to cancel.'

'Trust me, I'm an inventor,' Dr Trifle said. 'I'll have an answer before the week is out.'

'Dr Trifle is a brilliant inventor,' Selby thought, 'but somehow I think this is all going to go terribly wrong.'

For the next week Selby watched as Dr Trifle worked on his new invention, this time in the backyard.

'This is the longest invention that Dr Trifle has ever invented!' Selby thought. 'It stretches all the way from the back door to the fence. I've never seen so many levers, knobs and dials in my life.'

Finally the invention was complete and Dr Trifle stood in his best suit and tie next to the strange machine.

'I call it my Peep-Dipper,' he announced.

'Your what?' Mrs Trifle said.

'Well it's like a *sheep* dipper only it's for *people* so I could call it a People-Dipper. But I like just plain *Peep*-Dipper,' Dr Trifle explained.

'How does it work?'

'Pretend that I've just driven fifty kilometres over dusty roads and I'm covered in dirt.'

'You look perfectly clean to me,' said Mrs Trifle.

'We'll soon change that,' the doctor said, tipping a bucket of dirt over himself. 'Is that better? Okay, here we go. First I'll throw this switch.'

'My goodness, that's incredibly noisy,' Mrs Trifle said, putting her fingers in her ears.

'I beg your pardon?'

'I SAID IT'S VERY NOISY!'

'WHAT?!'

'NEVER MIND!'

Selby and Mrs Trifle watched as Dr Trifle stepped onto the conveyor belt and was thrown headfirst into a trough of water. When he came out, he was squeezed between ten huge soft wheels covered in bath towels. After that he was blasted with hot air.

'Ta-da!' he cried, stepping out of the Peep-Dipper perfectly clean and dry but with his hair pointing every which way. 'May I have the pleasure of this dance, madam?' he said, putting out his hand.

'That's amazing!' Selby thought. 'I was wrong. It actually worked!'

'That's brilliant!' Mrs Trifle said. 'But where does the dirty water come out?'

'It doesn't. This machine is very environmentally friendly. It recycles the water back into the same tank so it gets used over and over again.'

'So all the dirt stays in the water,' Mrs Trifle said. 'By the time a hundred people have gone through there they'll be having mud baths.'

'She's got a point,' Selby thought.

'I've thought of that,' Dr Trifle said pulling out a tray marked DIRT. 'The Peep-Dipper filters the water and the dirt all ends up in the dirt tray. Good, hey.'

'Your invention is marvellous,' Mrs Trifle said. 'And we won't have to cancel the Farmer's Fancy Dress Charity Ball after all.'

Later that day, when the Trifles were out, Selby just had to try out the marvellous machine. So he turned it on, and jumped on the conveyor belt.

'This is as much fun as a water slide!' Selby cried as he was catapulted into the water and then dragged through the drying rollers. 'But hang on, I'm not getting squozen dry. The rollers are too far apart for a little dog like me. I'll have to squeeze them in.'

Selby came out dripping wet, ran around to the side of the machine, and began twiddling dials and pulling on all the levers to adjust the rollers.

'That should do it,' he thought. 'Now I'll turn up the air so that my fur gets perfectly dry.'

After two more goes and more twiddling and levering Selby came out sparkling clean and perfectly dry.

'Perfect,' Selby thought. 'If the whole world was run by people like Dr Trifle it would be a wonderful place. Come to think of it, it's not so bad the way it is.'

The next morning the Peep-Dipper was loaded on a council truck and unloaded at the front door of Bogusville Town Hall.

That night, as the guests arrived for the Charity Ball in their fancy dress, a dusty and

114

sweaty Mrs Trifle explained about the problems with the dance floor and showed them the Peep-Dipper.

At first they were quiet and then a woman yelled out, 'Come on, you pikers, after me!'

Dr Trifle turned on the machine and one by one the farmers lined up and went through it into the hall. Just to be good sports, Dr and Mrs Trifle went through last. Suddenly the machine was turned off and there was total silence.

'I wonder if it worked?' Selby thought. 'Why is everyone so quiet? I have a feeling that something's gone dreadfully wrong.'

Selby ran around the machine and into the hall only to be greeted by the strangest sight he'd ever seen: there in the hall were Dr and Mrs Trifle and a hundred and fifty others standing silently in nothing but their underwear.

'I-I don't know how this could have happened,' Dr Trifle said. 'The rollers were much too tight. They weren't supposed to pull our clothes off.'

'Oh, no!' Selby screamed in his brain. 'I forgot to un-twiddle the diddles and un-lever

the levers! The rollers were too tight and the air was too blasty! It's pulled off everyone's shoes and clothes! Oh, woe, it's all my fault and now everyone's going to blame Dr Trifle!'

'I am terribly terribly sorry,' Mrs Trifle said. 'My husband's inventions don't always work perfectly but —'

Suddenly there was a burst of applause.

'This is brilliant!' someone cried. 'I feel so fresh and cool and clean. And who needs all those hot clothes on a warm night like this?!'

'And our feet can't scratch the dance floor!' someone yelled as the music began. 'Because we don't even have our shoes on.'

'Well it's not exactly the way I'd planned it,' Dr Trifle said with a blush. 'But it seems to have solved the scratched floor problem.'

'Don't worry, dear,' Mrs Trifle said with a laugh. 'We'll just rename it the Farmers' *Casual* Dress Charity Ball. May I have the pleasure of this dance?'

'Certainly,' Dr Trifle said.

'And I'll bet that this year,' Selby thought as he peeked into the DIRT box at the piles of shoes, clothing and lots and lots of loose money from people's pockets, 'the Charity Ball raises more money than ever before!'

SELBY'S DOZE CODE

'These child-proof medicine bottles are getting harder and harder to open,' Mrs Trifle said, struggling with the top of an aspirin bottle. 'This one's not just *child*-proof, it's absolutely *adult*-proof.'

'The problem is that little kids are getting smarter and smarter and medicine bottle makers have to come up with trickier and trickier tops to keep ahead of them,' Dr Trifle said.

'Come to think of it, you invented a better medicine bottle top not long ago.'

'Yes. The Tricky Twist Medicine Bottle Company asked me to come up with a new one. I invented a whole new system based on a different principle. It's a real doozey, if I do say so myself. Almost no one could get the tops off. And Tricky Twist loved it!' Dr Trifle said proudly.

'Oh, I give up. This silly bottle top is making my headache worse,' Mrs Trifle said putting it back in the medicine cabinet. 'Goodness me! We have to be at Aunt Jetty's garden party straight away. You'd better change those grubby clothes and get into some respectable ones.'

Selby sneezed three sneezes as the Trifles drove away. He had a heavy cold and he felt terrible. His throat was sore, he had a fever, and he'd sneezed his way through a whole box of tissues.

'I hate being sick,' he thought. 'When Dr Trifle is sick he gets to lie around and Mrs Trifle brings him lots of hot drinks and goodies to eat. Nobody ever does that for me. I just have to suffer. It's not fair.'

Selby sneezed his way through the last of the tissues and then looked in the medicine cabinet.

'Now where's some medicine to stop my nose from running? Crumbs, there's nothing here,' Selby thought. 'I know, I'll ring the chemist shop and see if I can get them to bring some runny nose medicine.'

Selby picked up the telephone and dialled.

'I'll pretend I'm Mrs Trifle,' he thought. 'With a cold like this I won't even have to imitate her voice because everyone sounds weird when they have a cold.'

'Hello, Kline and Vine Pharmacy, Barry Kline speaking,' the voice said. 'How may I help you?'

Selby cleared his throat and then said, 'This is Mrs Trifle,' only it came out sounding more like 'Dizziz bizziz Trifle.'

'I beg your pardon? Oh, Mrs Trifle! What a strange voice you have.'

'Bardon be but I hab a bizerable code.'

'I beg your pardon?'

'I bill.'

'You bill? I'm sorry but I don't quite understand. Did you say that you *bill*? You don't bill us — we bill you.'

'I said, "Ibe . . . ill".'

'Oh, *I'm ill.* I mean, you're ill. Oh, sorry to hear it, Mrs Trifle. What can we do for you?'

'I deed sub bedicine.'

'You … deed … sub … bedicine,' the man repeated very slowly. 'If it's *deeds* you want you should be ringing an estate agent, not a chemist.'

'Dough.'

'Did you say, "dough"?'

'Dough — I mean yes.'

'We don't have dough here, Mrs Trifle. Have you thought of ringing the bakery? Or if it's a sub you're after you could ring the navy,' the chemist added with a giggle. 'Oh, sorry, that was a terrible joke.'

Selby could feel himself getting hotter and hotter as he struggled to make himself understood. He spoke as slowly and clearly as he could.

'I said, I … deed … sub … bedicine.'

'You're sick in bed, is that it?'

'Dough. I … deed … sub … bills.'

'You're still ill, is that it? Well, you can't expect to get better in a minute.'

'You don't understab — *I deed bills*!'

'Bills.'

'Diddle dings do put in by bouth.'

'"Diddle dings do put in by bouth." Hmmm,' the chemist said.

'Bills! Bills!'

'Oh, *pills*! Why didn't you say so? What sort of pills do you want?'

'He understands me at last!' Selby thought. 'Now let's see if he can understand this: *I deed somedink do keeb by doze frub ruddick.*'

'Now you've really lost me, Mrs Trifle.'

'I hab a ruddy doze!'

'Ruddy toes? Let's see now, ruddy — that means red, doesn't it? Red toes. I know, you've got athlete's foot! We can give you some powder for that.'

'Dough! — I bead, degative. Ibe got a code in da doze.'

'Code? I'm not a spy, I'm a chemist,' Mr Kline chuckled. 'Or do you want to doze? Maybe you need some sleeping pills. You'll need a prescription for those, I'm afraid.'

'You don't understab be,' Selby said with a sneeze.

'Someone stabbed you?'

'*I hab a code in da doze!*' Selby squealed.

'I know! You've got a cold in the nose and you want some pills for it, is that it?'

'Spot od.'

'Good. A bedicine company — I mean a *medicine* company — just sent me a sample of a new, super good runny nose medicine. You can be the first to try it. It's called *Super Snot Stop*. Not the prettiest name in the world but I guess it tells you what it does. There are two pills in the bottle. Just take one and your nose will stop running immediately. The pills are very strong. Anyway, don't bother getting out of bed, I'll swing by and drop the bottle in your letterbox.'

'Dank kew. You're berry kide.'

'Sorry?'

'I said, "You're berry kide,"' Selby repeated.

'Yes, that's my name, Barry Kline. Did you want something else?'

'Debbor bide.'

'Deborah Vine is my partner. Do you want to speak to her?'

'Dope.'

'Well, you could at least be polite about it. Just because I couldn't understand you doesn't mean I'm a dope. Goodness me, Mrs Trifle. Oh, well, I guess we all get a bit cranky when we're sick. I'll drop the pills around straight away.'

'Dank you.'

Click.

'Poor Mr Kline,' Selby thought. 'I hope I didn't hurt his feelings.'

Fifteen sneezes later Selby watched as the chemist dropped the bottle of pills in the letter-box and then drove away. In a second, Selby had snatched the *Super Snot Stop* bottle and brought it into the house.

'Thank goodness,' he thought. 'Now to get the top off this thing.'

Selby struggled with it for a minute without success.

'This must be another one of those child-proof thingies,' he thought. 'Maybe you have to push it down and then turn it.'

Selby pushed and turned and pulled and turned and even tried to slide it to the side but the bottle wouldn't open.

'This is driving me bonkers!' Selby thought. 'This isn't only child-proof and people-proof, it's even *pet*-proof! I'd ring Barry Kline again and ask him how to open it but it's no good — he'd never understand me.'

Selby threw the bottle on the hard kitchen floor only to have it bounce back up. He threw it again even harder and it bounced around the walls until it hit him on the head and dropped to the floor.

'Youch! I'll fix you!' Selby said with a sneeze. 'Where's Dr Trifle's big rock-smashing hammer?'

But before Selby could even think to blink he heard two big sneezes — and neither of them was his. He spun around to see Dr and Mrs Trifle coming through the door.

'No wonder I had a headache,' Mrs Trifle said. 'It was a cold coming on. Now I'm — *ah-choo!* — all sneezy.'

'Me — *choo!* — too,' Dr Trifle said.

'But look!' Mrs Trifle exclaimed, picking up the medicine bottle. 'It's that new *Super Snot Stop* that's had all the ads on TV. Where did it come from?'

'I have no idea. I don't remember buying it.'

'You don't remember lots of things, dear. But never mind, let's see if it works as well as it's supposed to.'

'You'll never find out because you'll never

get the lid off,' Selby thought as he watched Mrs Trifle struggling with the bottle top.

'Here, let me try,' Dr Trifle said, taking the bottle and opening it easily.

'Crumbs,' Selby thought. 'How'd he do that?'

'How'd you do that?' Mrs Trifle asked.

'First I pressed down, then I turned it one turn in the wrong direction, and then I pulled up and pushed it to the side. Nothing to it,' Dr Trifle said, popping a pill into his mouth and handing the other to Mrs Trifle.

'But how on earth did you know to do that?'

'Simple: the bottle top is based on my new system — the one I came up with for the Tricky Twist Medicine Bottle Company,' Dr Trifle said. 'Hmmm, this *Super Snot Stop* is great. I can feel my sniffles disappearing already.'

'So can I,' Mrs Trifle said. 'But tell me, how is anyone else supposed to figure out how to get the top off the bottle?'

'Well you know how I said that little kids were getting smarter and smarter?' Dr Trifle asked.

'Yes.'

'Well they still can't read,' Dr Trifle explained. 'And the directions about how to take the bottle top off are written on the label. Nothing to it.'

'Goodness me,' Mrs Trifle said. 'You're right. It's all written right here. I guess I would have noticed it sooner or later.'

'I can't believe it,' Selby thought as he sneezed another sneeze and crept away to lie down. 'The one thing I could have done — read the label — I didn't do. I give up.'

SELBY'S HIGH Q

Selby's worst nightmare had come true. He was in a special laboratory being studied by a scientist.

It all began when Mrs Trifle's cousin Wilhemina came to town to judge the Bogusville Canine Society's annual dog show. As usual she stayed with the Trifles. When she went off in the morning she left a page torn out of a magazine lying on the coffee table. Later, when Selby was alone, he noticed it and read the writing at the top: *Check Your Dog's IQ.*

'An IQ test,' Selby said, grabbing a pencil and writing his name at the top of the form. 'I've always wanted to test my IQ. Hmmm, I wonder what IQ stands for. I know it has something to do with intelligence. That must be the *I* bit. I wonder about the *Q*. Let's see how I go.'

One by one, Selby read through the questions: *Can your dog sit?* He quickly ticked the box that said 'Yes'. *Can your dog shake hands?* Yes. *Roll over?* Yes. *Does your dog know left from right?* Yes, of course. *Does your dog know which way is up?* Yes. If I didn't, how could I get up in the morning? Stupid question. *Can your dog chase sticks and bring them back?* Yes — if I feel like it. *Does your dog know where his food is kept?* Yes, of course, you nong. Every dog knows that. *Does your dog like music?* Yes.

Selby continued ticking the answers as the questions got harder and harder. The final question was: *Does your dog know the sound of your car's engine?* 🐾 'Not really, but I'm going to say yes anyway,' Selby thought.

Selby finished the quiz and then added up the score.

'One hundred and ten,' he said. 'Let's see what category that puts me in. Oh, good. "Dog Genius." Absolutely true, if I do say so myself.'

🐾 *Paw note: Some dogs do know the sound of their owners' car engines. Not me. I'm not into cars.* S

Selby was about to erase all his answers when suddenly Cousin Wilhemina opened the front door and dashed into the loungeroom.

'Where did I leave that thing?' she said, looking around. 'Oh, there it is.'

Wilhemina grabbed the IQ test and was about to dash out again when she glanced down at it and stopped in her tracks.

'Someone's already filled it in,' she said. 'It must have been Dr Trifle. Hmmm, one hundred and ten! Wow! I wonder which dog he was testing. Surely not old dumb dumb here,' she said looking over at Selby. 'Good grief! The Trifles only have one dog it must be him! *One hundred and ten! Unbelievable!* And all these years I thought he was too dumb to come in out of the rain.'

Cousin Wil looked at Selby and then her face lit up.

'Come with me, pooch,' she said, grabbing him by the collar. 'I'm going to get you tested properly.'

'What have I done?' Selby thought as the woman dragged him into her car. 'I may be super smart but filling out that dog IQ test was the stupidest thing I've ever done!'

Within minutes Cousin Wilhemina was pulling Selby into the Dog IQ Testing Tent at the dog show and handing his IQ test to a startled Dog Resources scientist. The woman looked over the form for a moment and then looked up.

'I can't believe it!' she exclaimed. 'We get a few smart dogs but this little guy is smarter than I am!'

'That wouldn't be difficult,' Selby thought.

'Are you sure this is true?' the scientist asked. 'Are you sure someone wasn't just playing a joke on you?'

'Well it was filled out by either Dr or Mrs Trifle and they wouldn't joke about a thing like this,' Cousin Wil said. 'Unless you believe that the dog filled it out himself,' she added with a long, screaming laugh.

'Oh, yes, that's a good one,' the scientist laughed back. 'Then I guess we can only do one thing.'

'What is that?'

'I'll have to send him off to the National Dog Testing Laboratory in Canberra to be studied by the best Dog Resources scientists in the country. Do you have any idea what a terrific sheep dog a fellow like this would make? Why, he could not only round up the sheep but shear them too. But forget shearing: he could do almost anything a human could do. We could breed a whole race of hard-working, super-smart dogs and then we people could sit back and take it easy while the dogs did all the work.'

'That's what you think,' Selby thought. 'Oh, woe, how will I ever get out of this?'

'But I'd better do another quick test just to make sure before I ship him to Canberra,' the scientist said.

A tiny smile formed at the corners of Selby's mouth. He watched patiently as the scientist placed two bowls on the floor — one was empty and one was filled with wonderful smelling food.

'I'll play dumb,' Selby thought as he licked the empty bowl, 'and I'll be back home in a few minutes.'

'Hmmm, that's very strange,' Cousin Wil said. 'I would've thought that even the dumbest dog would go for the food.'

'Not necessarily,' the scientist said. 'This is why it takes an expert like me to check these results. A very smart dog might be very particular about his food. This might not be the sort of food he likes. By licking the empty bowl he's sending a clear message to us that he wants better food or nothing at all.'

'How interesting,' Cousin Wil said.

'If you think that was interesting,' Selby thought. 'Just wait.'

For the next fifteen minutes the scientist gave Selby test after test. When she told him to sit he just stared at her. When she put out her hand and said, 'Shake!' he licked it. When she tried to get him to roll over, he got halfway over and then lay on his back pretending to sleep. The tests went on and on with Selby failing every one.

'Now for the rain test,' she said.

'The rain test?' Cousin Wil asked.

'Yes, watch.'

The scientist got out a kennel and put it next to Selby. Next she turned on a garden hose and pointed it up in the air. Selby just sat there letting the freezing water soak him.

'The dumbest thing I can think of doing is to just stand here instead of going into that nice,

dry, warm doghouse,' he thought. 'And that's what I'm going to do even if I catch pneumonia! I'm going to fail this test even if it kills me!'

Finally the scientist shook her head and turned off the water.

'I'm terribly sorry,' Cousin Wilhemina said finally. 'Whoever filled out that form must have been joking. Selby is as thick as a brick. We won't waste your time any longer. Come along, Selby.'

'I knew that if I really used my brain I could fail,' Selby thought. 'I hope she takes me home straight away. I can't stand dog shows.'

'Waste my time? Are you kidding? This is fantastic!' the scientist shrieked. 'This calls for some serious testing.'

'But why would you want to test a dog that's obviously as dull as ditchwater?' Cousin Wil asked.

'The point is that in order to get our dog IQ tests right we need to test dogs that are really smart, of course, but we also need at least one that's an absolute bonehead. And this dog is the biggest numbskull I've ever come across. Why he doesn't even have enough sense to come in out of the rain! I'm going to send him off to the National Dog Testing Lab in Canberra for a year of testing!'

'What have I done?!' Selby thought. 'I shouldn't have tried to fail *everything*. I should have just tried to be average. I don't want to be tested by stupid scientists for a whole year! They might even keep me for another year! Maybe I should talk to this nitwit in plain English and explain what I did and why I did it. What am I saying?! Then they'd want to keep me forever!'

Suddenly a voice boomed behind Selby.

'Did I hear you say that you wanted to send Selby somewhere for testing? You'll do no such thing!'

There, standing in the doorway, was Mrs Trifle looking very angry.

'Why have you brought Selby here? Cousin Wil,' she demanded.

'I-I-I because he was smart,' her cousin stammered. 'Only it turns out he's really very stupid.'

'Don't be silly,' Mrs Trifle said, grabbing Selby's collar. 'He's not smart and he's not stupid. He's just normal and I'm not having him sent away anywhere. Come along home, Selby.'

'Oh, thank you for rescuing me!' Selby thought, breathing a sigh of relief as he trotted after Mrs Trifle. 'I'm never going to take another one of those silly tests again. I still don't know what IQ stands for but for me it means *I quit*!'

SELBY DOOMED

Selby's secret was out.

Well, nearly out. Selby was one mouse click from ruin. In a fraction of a second, Selby's secret would be there on the computer screen in huge letters for the Trifles to see. Mrs Trifle cupped her hand over the mouse and started to click.

Selby waited for the terrible moment. He closed his eyes. Hot tears ran down his cheeks. His body shuddered. He began to whimper and whine.

'Gulp. This is it,' he thought. 'My carefree life is over. Goodbye freedom. Goodbye peace and quiet. Hello being all over TV all the time. Hello not being able to walk down the street without people talking to me. Hello having to be studied by scientists. Hello having to *work*! Oh woe woe woe.'

It all happened the day he found a hidden doorway and creaked his way down the rickety staircase to the Dungeon of Doom.

'Now to find the key to the Dark Chamber. If I find that maybe I can find the Celestial Treasure Chest too!' Selby thought. 'Doom Avengers is such a great computer game! I can't stop playing it! I think of it night and day. Every time I close my eyes it's there. If the Trifles stay away for another hour maybe I can get to Level Two. Oh, boy!'

Selby moved the mouse, slowly searching the dungeon. There was a painting of a windmill on one wall, and a bookcase filled with books on another. On the floor was a sword and a rocking horse.

'The key must be here somewhere,' Selby said, moving the arrow around the screen and clicking on everything in sight.

The windmill in the painting turned and then stopped. The sword sent off glittering rays, and the rocking horse rocked forward and back.

Suddenly a deep voice said:

Here's a clue for Level Two:
If you can read then you'll succeed.

'Read? Succeed?' Selby thought. 'I know!'

Selby moved the pointer over the bookcase, clicking frantically. Finally a book fell to the floor and opened.

'There it is!' Selby gasped. 'The key to the Dark Chamber!'

Selby used the pointer to put the key in the lock. With a creak the door opened.

Clever you, you've reached Level Two
Now let's see if you can get to Level Three.

'Oh, goody!' Selby thought as he looked around. 'Now for the Celestial Treasure Chest. Where could it be? In the mummy case? Maybe I have to unwrap the mummy. Or could it be something to do with the bottles in the wine rack? Maybe I'm supposed to pull down the chandelier.'

Selby was so caught up in the game that he didn't notice that the Trifles had returned.

Suddenly Mrs Trifle peered in the door of the study.

'Selby!' she screamed. 'What are you doing?'

Selby froze. His fur stood on end. His ears were as hot as match heads.

'Oh, no!' he thought. 'She's caught me using the computer! This is it! Why did I ever get hooked on this stupid game?!'

'What's wrong?' Dr Trifle called.

'Come quickly!' Mrs Trifle yelled. 'Selby is at the computer. Look!'

Selby's mind raced like the hands of a broken clock.

'She can't see that the computer is on from where she's standing,' he thought. 'For all she knows I'm just sitting in the chair *in front of* the computer. I've got to turn this thing off without her seeing. And I've got to do it *fast!*'

Selby's paw quietly pressed the OFF button shutting down the computer. But just as it went off these words flashed on the screen and then disappeared:

SELBY IS THE NEW MASTER

'Oh, no!' he thought. 'I must have typed my real name when I started the game! I should have just made up a name! I didn't know it was going to do this!'

'What a hoot,' Mrs Trifle said as she and Dr Trifle came around the desk. 'Selby looks like he's actually using the computer — but of course that's impossible.'

'We should get a photo of him sitting here.'

'Forget the photo,' Mrs Trifle said. 'You forgot why we raced home. We've got to have another go at Doom Avengers. I love that game!'

'Me too. Let's boot it up,' said Dr Trifle. 'Come on, Selby, get down from there.'

Selby climbed down and lay on the carpet in a panic.

'That was *soooo* close!' he thought. 'But it's not over yet. If they don't get further along in the game than I did it'll say SELBY IS STILL THE MASTER when they quit. Then they'll know that I was playing with the computer and they'll put two and two together and then they'll know my secret!'

'Let's pick up the game from where we left off, okay?' Mrs Trifle said. 'I don't want to start from the beginning again.'

Selby watched as the Trifles fumbled their way through the Magic Maze to the hidden door behind the Fantasy Fountain.

'How do we open the door?' Dr Trifle asked. 'There's no key and there's no doorknob. We're stuck.'

'Just knock the knocker, for heaven's sake!' Selby thought. 'It's simple!'

'Maybe we should try knocking the knocker,' Mrs Trifle said.

'I don't know,' Dr Trifle cautioned. 'Remember, if you do the wrong thing sometimes you end up back at the beginning again. Maybe we should think of a reason why we should be knocking the knocker before we do it.'

'You're right,' Mrs Trifle said. 'Let's just quit and come back later.'

'Forget the reasons!' Selby thought. 'Just go ahead! Don't be so scared. Try things! It's only a game. Please don't quit now!'

'Oh! Let's live dangerously,' Mrs Trifle said. 'I

can't stand the suspense. I've got to try the knocker.'

Selby breathed a sigh of relief as the door opened and the Trifles made their way down the staircase and into the Dungeon of Doom.

Once again the voice said:

Here's a clue for Level Two:
If you can read then you'll succeed.

'Hmmm,' Dr Trifle hmmmed. 'These clues are too confusing. Of course we know how to read but what does that have to do with anything?'

For fifteen minutes Selby watched as the Trifles tried everything in the room. Finally, just as they were about to give up, they touched the book in the bookcase and out came the book and the key. In a minute they were inside the Dark Chamber.

The deep voice spoke again:

Clever you, you've reached Level Two
Now let's see if you can get to Level Three.

Mrs Trifle tried and tried to find the Celestial Treasure Chest without success.

'Oh, I give up,' she said. 'And I'm hungry. Let's close it down and come back after lunch.'

'Any minute now they'll stop the game and the sign will flash on and give my secret away,' Selby thought.

Selby waited for the terrible moment. He closed his eyes. Hot tears ran down his cheeks. His body shuddered. He began to whimper and whine.

'Gulp. This is it,' he thought.

Dr Trifle looked away from the computer screen.

'Goodness,' he said. 'Selby must be having a bad dream. He's-he's sort of whining. I've never heard him whine before. He must be sick. I think we should take him to the vet.'

'I think we're onto something here,' Mrs Trifle said, staring at the computer screen.

'You didn't hear a word I said, did you?' Dr Trifle said.

'Please darling, could it wait? I'm really into this.'

'But Selby could be sick. Would you please listen to me?'

'I'm listening, I'm listening. I'll be with you in a second,' Mrs Trifle said moving the pointer to the wine rack. 'Please don't spoil my concentration.'

Suddenly a bottle moved out and there was a loud *clong*! as the wine rack slid aside. There behind it was the Celestial Treasure Chest.

More more more! You're heading for Level Four. If you stay alive, you could reach Level Five.

'Now that's enough,' Dr Trifle said. 'You're getting hooked on this silly game. It's not good for you. Let's have some lunch, okay?'

'That's fine with me,' Mrs Trifle said, clicking the mouse to stop the game. With this, this sign came up:

MRS TRIFLE IS THE NEW MASTER

'You're a very clever person,' Dr Trifle said. 'How did you know to pull out that bottle in the wine rack?'

'Me? You were the one who said it.'

'No, I didn't.'

'Yes, you did. You said something about wine.'

'No, no,' Dr Trifle laughed. 'I said I'd never heard Selby whine before. Wh-wh-*whine*, not *wine*. I knew you weren't listening to me.'

'Sorry, dear,' Mrs Trifle said. 'But look, Selby seems okay now. Why he's as happy as Larry.'

'I'm happier than Larry,' Selby thought. 'I'm as happy as *Selby*!'

SELBY SPRUNG

'The program showing the highlights of yesterday's Bush Olympics is about to come on TV,' Selby thought. 'I wish the Trifles would hurry up and go out so I can watch it.'

'The Reynolds are usually on time,' Mrs Trifle said to Dr Trifle as they sat reading the morning newspaper. 'Where could they be?'

'I'm sure they'll be here soon,' Dr Trifle said, turning to the sports page. 'Goodness me! Look how well Bogusville did in the Bush Olympics. Do you know who won the pole vault?'

'No, I don't,' Mrs Trifle said.

'Neither do I!' Selby thought, clamping his paws over his ears. 'And I don't want to know! I want to see it on TV and be surprised!'

Selby waited till Dr Trifle's mouth stopped moving and then uncovered his ears.

'It's the results of the javelin we should know,' Mrs Trifle said.

'Sorry?'

'The javelin. That spear thingy that you throw.'

'I know what a javelin is. Hmmm, I'll see if the results are here,' Dr Trifle said, scanning the sports page. 'Goodness me! Guess who won?! It was —'

'No!' Selby thought, covering his ears again. 'Don't tell me! I've got to get out of here.'

No sooner had Selby gone out to the backyard than the Trifles' friends arrived and they all drove off together. Selby tore back into the house, turned on the TV, and then got himself a bowl of goodies to nibble before returning to the loungeroom.

'Oh good!' he said, talking to himself out loud. 'It's only just begun! Look! The men's pole vault is about to start.'

Selby watched as Postie Paterson took a long run up and then plunged the pole into the ground, sending himself high up into the air and just clearing the bar.

'Great jump, Postie!' Selby yelled. 'No one will beat that!'

Selby crammed a pawful of chips into his mouth. Then, just as the second pole vaulter was making his run, Selby heard a noise behind him. It wasn't just a noise but a *voice*!

'Excuse me,' the voice said. 'But who are you?'

Selby spun around to see a teenage girl sitting in a chair at the back of the room.

'Who's that?!' Selby thought, his heart skipping a beat. 'What's she doing here?!'

'Sorry if I startled you,' the girl said.

'Oh, no,' Selby thought. 'She saw me talking! She *heard* me talking! Why didn't I look before I turned on the TV?'

'Why are you so quiet? Cat got your tongue?'

'She knows my secret!' Selby thought. 'It's no use. I can't pretend any longer.'

'Hello,' Selby said out loud.

'Are you a friend of the Trifles?'

'A friend? Well, I guess you could say that. I've known them for a long long time.'

Slowly Selby felt his panic go away.

'This is weird,' he thought. 'She's so matter-of-fact about it. I guess I should have known that sooner or later someone would catch me talking but I never thought it was going to be like this. I always thought they'd scream or faint or just run away — maybe all three at once. She seems all relaxed. It makes me feel relaxed too.'

'This is funny,' the girl laughed. 'I guess the Trifles have been keeping you a secret.'

'I'm the one who's been keeping me a secret,' he said.

'I beg your pardon.'

'I said, "I'm the one who's been keeping me a secret,"' Selby said. 'They didn't know. They don't — even to this day. You're the first and the only one.'

The girl looked at Selby and then laughed.

'You're weird,' she said.

'Well I guess I am a little out of the ordinary.'

'That is funny.'

'It is?' Selby said. 'By the way, who are you?'

'Oh, I'm sorry I didn't introduce myself. I'm Chelsea Reynolds. My parents are with the Trifles.'

'And they left you here?'

'I asked if I could just stay and read a book,' the girl said, holding up the open book that lay in her lap. 'I thought it might be boring listening to a lot of grown-up talk. Besides, it's a great book. I can't put it down.'

Suddenly Selby heard the TV announcer's voice.

'And now we go to the women's javelin throw. We cross to Vicki Grant at trackside. What's happening there, Vicks?'

'Please excuse me,' Selby said, 'but if I'm sort of . . .'

'Sort of what?'

'Well confused, I guess. I should have known that sooner or later I'd be found out.'

'Found out?'

'Well you have to admit that it's not normal,' Selby said. 'Me talking like this and all. You must be a bit surprised.'

'We've had some great throws today, Larry, but I think this could be the big one,' the other TV announcer said.

'Would you mind awfully,' the girl said to Selby, 'if we watch this?'

'No worries. That's why I turned on the TV, Chelsea. Do you mind if I call you Chelsea?'

'Of course not.'

Selby watched as a girl of about Chelsea's age ran up to a white line and stopped abruptly, hurling a javelin far out into a field.

'*Wonderful throw!*' Vicki cried. '*They're measuring it now but I don't think it's quite made it.*'

Selby looked at Chelsea then turned and looked out the window.

'This is bizarre,' he thought. 'Okay, everything seems fine. But what now? What do I do next? It's great that Chelsea didn't freak out but this has to be the end of my wonderful peaceful life.' Selby shook his head in amazement. 'Maybe when Chelsea tells the Trifles they won't freak out either. Maybe *no one will care.*'

A little movie began to play in Selby's mind. A TV newsreader was almost at the end of the news when he said, 'Here are a couple of stories to warm every heart. The first one comes from Bogusville, a country town here in Australia. Yesterday the mayor of that tiny town discovered that her dog, Selby, can actually talk.

That's right, he speaks perfect English. In what is thought to be a world first this talkative little terrier, this wire-haired wordsmith, this chattering chihuahua, gave a speech to the citizens of that fair town telling about himself and how he acquired his gift of the gab.' As the newsreader continued, Selby saw a film clip of himself talking to the citizens of Bogusville. 'At the end of his talk,' the newsreader went on, 'this daring little dachshund asked that his privacy be respected and that he be allowed to live his life in peace — which, of course, everyone was happy to do. Our second story comes from a toy company where they've invented a mechanical cat so lifelike that no one can tell the difference between it and the real thing. It just lies on the lounge all day, not moving a muscle, and purrs when you pat it. This minimum-maintenance moggy should make a purrrrrrfect Christmas gift.'

'I've been worried all these years for nothing,' Selby thought. 'When the Trifles get home I'm going to tell them everything. No more pretending. No more trying to cover things up. No more narrow escapes.'

Selby watched two more javelin throwers make their throws.

'*And now here comes last year's title holder,*' Vicki said. '*She's making her run-up. Look at that girl go! And now she lets it fly! This could be the one.*'

Selby watched as the javelin flew through the air and finally stuck into the ground. Again people in white jackets came running out to measure the distance.

'*That's it!*' Vicki cried. '*Chelsea Reynolds has made the best throw of the day!*'

'Chelsea Reynolds?' Selby said. 'But that's you. Of course it's you! I can see that it's you!'

'Well, yes,' the girl said, blushing.

'Did you win?' Selby asked.

'Well just listen,' Chelsea said.

'*So for the second year in a row,*' Vicki said, '*Chelsea takes out the javelin title! What a wonderful effort. And to think, she's been blind since birth.*'

'Congratulations!' Selby said.

'Thanks,' the girl said.

'Hang on!' Selby said. 'Blind? Did she say that you have been blind all your life?'

'That's right.'

'Well that changes everything.'

'What do you mean?'

'Nothing. I mean it must be very difficult —'

'Not really,' the girl interrupted. 'Blind people can do a lot more than you think.'

'Well, yes, but it must be terrible,' Selby said, 'being blind.'

'No, it's not terrible. It's okay. Well it's normal for me anyway.'

'But that book —'

The girl laughed. 'It's written in braille, silly,' she said, holding it up so that Selby could see the little bumps on the page. 'You just read it with your fingertips.'

'But you watch TV,' Selby said.

'*Everyone* watches TV,' the girl said, 'even blind people. But enough about me, tell me something about yourself.'

'Well I ... well ... I ...'

'What do you look like?'

'What do I look like? What *do* I look like? What do *I* look like? Hmmm. Let me see now.'

'Well? Are you tall? Short?'

'Well I'm — I'm short. But not too short. Sort of tall, actually. And I'm quite good looking. Do you know the film star Dino diSwarve?'

'Yes, of course, everyone knows Dino diSwarve. They say he's a real spunk.'

'People often mistake us on the street. It's embarrassing. Women keep trying to kiss me.'

'They do?'

'Sadly, yes,' Selby sighed. 'I have to fight them off. It gets very boring. I have to wear sunnies and pull my hat down over my face so they can't see me properly.'

'Now I know you're kidding,' the girl laughed. 'You do have a good sense of humour.'

'I do?'

'You do.'

'Well, thanks.'

'Do you know any jokes?'

'Let me think,' Selby said, trying to remember one of Gary Gaggs' jokes. 'What do you get if you feed a cat lemons?'

'I don't know. What do you get?'

'A sour puss. Get it? A *sour* puss. Woo! Woo! Woo!' Selby said, adding the woo woo woos that Gary always said at the end of his jokes.

Chelsea laughed long and loud.

'That's a good one. Do you know another one?'

'An angel went up to another angel and said, "Halo",' Selby said. 'Get it? Halo? Woo! Woo! Woo!'

'That's great!' Chelsea said. 'Do you know any more?'

Suddenly Selby heard a noise behind him.

'Well, Chelsea, I see you've got company,' Mrs Trifle said.

Selby turned to see the Trifles and Chelsea's parents coming through the front door.

'Oh, no!' Selby thought. 'I should have kept an eye out! What am I going to do now?!'

'Yes,' Chelsea said, 'we've just been having a nice chat, haven't we? Sorry, what's your name?'

'A chat?' Mrs Trifle said. 'You were talking to Selby?'

'Selby? Oh, is that your name?'

The Trifles were silent for a second and then Dr Trifle said, 'Selby is a dog, Chelsea. I doubt that you were talking to him.'

'Then who was I talking to? Who was telling me those corny jokes?'

'I certainly don't know. There's no one here but us and Selby.'

'Then he must have left just before you

arrived,' Chelsea said. 'It's funny that he didn't say goodbye.'

'Did you say that he told you corny jokes?' Mrs Trifle asked.

'Yes and he said, "Woo! Woo! Woo!" after them. He said he was an old friend of yours.'

'Gary Gaggs!' Mrs Trifle said. 'It's a pity we didn't arrive a bit earlier. I would have liked to see him. Just our luck, I guess.'

'And it was my luck too that you didn't,' Selby thought. 'Only mine was *good* luck. What a relief!'

SELBY SUBMERGED

Selby plunged over the side of the boat, hurtling through the air until his front paws parted the water. For a moment he saw nothing but a veil of tiny bubbles. Then, there it was just below him. He snatched at the necklace but it was no use. It was too far away now and sinking fast. He watched the glitter of gemstones disappear into the murky depths of the deepest trench in the deepest ocean in all the world.

Selby gagged, trying to hang on to the precious air that still filled his lungs. He looked up to the surface of the water far above him.

Suddenly it hit him.

'Why am I here?' he thought. 'What have I

done?! Why am I trying to rescue a billion dollar necklace from the sea *when I don't even know how to swim*?!'

On the boat above, unaware of Selby's predicament, Dr and Mrs Trifle sipped cups of hot cocoa.

'We're so lucky to be alive,' Mrs Trifle said, wrapping a blanket around herself.

'Yes ...' Dr Trifle stopped to shiver and then continued, 'and so is Selby, don't forget. He's been such a wonderful friend to us all these years. Sometimes I think we've taken him too much for granted. By the way where is he?'

'I don't know,' Mrs Trifle said. 'He was here a minute ago. He's probably crawled off to take a nap somewhere. I'm sure he's okay.'

Selby thrashed about with his paws, clawing the water the way he'd seen dogs do when they dog-paddled, struggling towards the surface. But he knew that this time he'd gone too far. Even if someone discovered that he'd gone overboard, there wasn't enough time to be rescued.

Just as Selby ran out of energy and stopped paddling he saw a huge dark shape in the water beginning to circle.

'Oh, no!' he screamed. His words disappeared in the silence of a huge bubble. 'Shark! Help! Someone save me! Oh, please, please don't let me die!'

> Author's note: Read on and you'll see how Selby got into this predicament and what happened next. But I'm warning you: don't read this last Selby story unless you're feeling very strong. If you do: make sure you have a box of tissues handy.

This tragic tale began one day when Dr Trifle's old ocean scientist friend, Dr Septimus C. Squirt, asked him to help collect some tiny sea creatures.

'Isn't that a job for one of those scooba-dooba people?' Dr Trifle asked. 'Or maybe one of those little submarine deep diving doovers?'

'Goodness, no!' exclaimed the scientist. 'These sea creatures live at the very bottom of the deepest, most dangerous trench in the deepest ocean in all the world. No human being has ever been down that far. Well except the people who went down in the *S. S. Humungous* many years ago. Anyway, no one's been down and come back up alive. Even the best bathyscaphe — or deep diving doover, as you call it — would crumple like aluminium foil at those depths.'

'The *Humungous*,' Dr Trifle said, letting out a low whistle. 'The huge passenger ship that sank with everyone on board. It's never been found, has it?'

'Nope.'

'If someone could find it they could find that necklace — the Billion Dollar Bobble.'

'Bobble schmobble,' Dr Squirt said. 'I didn't come here to talk about boring old sunken ships and boring necklaces. What I'm after is *Flashipodicus*! Yeeeeeeeeeesssssssss!'

'*Flashipodicus*?'

'*Flashipodicae deepyensis* to give them their proper name. Little animals that live down there. We usually just call them Flash-Greebies because of the way their bodies light up so they can see their way around in the dark. We only know they exist because sometimes a dead one floats to the surface. No one has ever caught a live one. I want to catch a lot of them to study them properly.'

'The *S. S. Humungous*,' Selby thought. 'The great lost ship that has never been found. It gives me the shivers just to think of it sitting in the darkness on the bottom of the sea. Sheeeeesh! It makes my fur stand on end. Who would want to go down there? Double sheeeeesh!'

'So how can I help you collect these Flash-Greebies?' Dr Trifle asked his old friend.

'Build me a deep diving doover that's strong enough so it won't crumple down there. How about it?'

'That sounds like fun,' Dr Trifle said. 'I'll give it a go.'

So it was that week after week Selby watched Dr Trifle build the tiny submarine which he named the *Sea Squirt* after Dr Septimus C. Squirt. And soon Selby found himself on a big boat along with Dr Squirt and the Trifles heading towards the deepest trench in the deepest ocean in all the world. And it wasn't long before they were ready to hoist the *Sea Squirt* over the side and into the depths.

'Okay, who's going down in it?' Dr Squirt asked, rubbing his hands together with excitement. 'Someone has to actually collect the critters.'

'Well you are, aren't you?' Mrs Trifle said.

'Not me. I have to stay here and twiddle the dials on the instruments and make sure you get down to the right place and everything.'

'Why don't I twiddle the instruments and you catch the critters?' Dr Trifle asked.

'Because I'm the expert twiddler,' Dr Squirt explained. 'Don't tell me you're a scaredy-cat.'

'Well . . . no but —'

'But nothing. In you go. Come on, time's a-wasting.'

Dr and Mrs Trifle looked at each other for a moment.

'Come on, dear,' Mrs Trifle said. 'I'll come too. We'll even bring Selby. It'll be like a family outing. I'm sure we'll be perfectly safe in your invention. You're such a good inventor.'

'I am? I mean, of course I am. Well, okay.'

'No, no, no, I don't want to go!' Selby screamed in his brain. 'I hate water! I hate deep water even more! The deeper it is, the more I hate it! And this is the deepest trench in the deepest ocean in all the world!'

'Okay, in you go, boy,' Dr Trifle said, and before Selby knew it he was in the *Sea Squirt* with the Trifles descending into the darkness.

'I can't see anything,' Mrs Trifle said. 'Turn on the headlight.'

Dr Trifle turned on the light and Selby and the Trifles peered through the portholes down into the depths. An hour passed and then a long, thin edge of rock appeared out of the black below.

'That must be the bottom,' Mrs Trifle said.

Dr Squirt's voice crackled over the radio.

'You're not at the bottom yet,' he said. 'It's probably just the peak of a submerged mountain range.'

'Sheeeeesh!' Selby thought. 'Mountain peaks at the bottom of the sea. This really gives me the willies.'

The *Sea Squirt* continued down past rocky mountain peaks so covered in white sand that it looked like snow. Finally they reached the bottom of the trench.

'What do we do now?' Dr Trifle asked over the radio. 'I don't see any Greebies.'

'Turn off your light,' Dr Squirt said.

Mrs Trifle turned off the light. In a minute they saw pinpoints of light moving about on the ocean bottom.

'Greebies ahoy!' Mrs Trifle cried. 'This is so exciting!'

'Okay,' Dr Squirt said. 'Pick them up and plonk them in the jar. When it's full, I'll pull you back up.'

Mrs Trifle started the motor and guided the *Sea Squirt* along the ocean bottom. Dr Trifle stretched his arms out into the hollow arms that stuck out in front of the submarine. One of them had a jar in it. With the other he picked up a Flash-Greebie.

'This is really spooky,' Selby thought as he looked out through half-closed eyes. 'But it's fun. At least we didn't get crumpled.'

Mrs Trifle guided the *Sea Squirt* along in the blackness as Dr Trifle collected the little animals. Suddenly there was a scraping noise.

'I wonder what that could be,' Mrs Trifle said, turning on the light. 'We seem to be in a cave or something. Look! There's something round on the bottom right in front of us. Pick it up and see what it is.'

Dr Trifle picked it up and shook the sand off it.

'It's a dinner plate!' he said. 'Look it's got writing on it! It says "S. S. HUMUNGOUS". Good gracious!' he called out into the microphone. 'Somehow we've found our way into the wreck of the *Humungous*!'

'Have you filled the jar yet?' Dr Squirt asked.

'No, not yet. These little beasties are so small that it'll take forever to fill it. Aren't you excited about the ship?'

'I'm a scientist, not one of those people who goes around collecting useless junk from old shipwrecks,' Dr Squirt said. 'What do you say I pull you back up and we call it a day.'

'Hang on! Let me get this thing out of the *Humungous* first!' Mrs Trifle said. 'Don't pull yet!'

But it was too late and suddenly the *Sea Squirt* lurched violently, smashing against a rusty steel wall and breaking its light before stopping.

'I beg your pardon?' Dr Squirt said. 'What did you say?'

'We said, "Don't pull yet",' Dr Trifle sighed. 'Now we're stuck in here.'

'Oooops. Okay, so find your way back out and then I'll pull you up.'

'We can't find our way anywhere!' Mrs Trifle said. 'We can't see a thing! You broke our light when you tried to pull us up.'

'Ooops, sorry about that,' Dr Squirt said. 'I'll make it up to you.'

'How will you do that when we can't get back to the surface?'

'It's just an expression,' Dr Squirt said. 'You don't suppose there's some way you could attach the bottle of Flash-Greebies to the cable and I could at least rescue them?'

'No there isn't!' Mrs Trifle exclaimed.

'Okay don't get angry. No harm in asking.'

Selby's heart started beating like a bongo drum. Sweat poured down his face as Mrs Trifle tried and tried to find the way out of the wreck. Every time she went in one direction she bumped into a wall or ceiling.

'It's no use,' she said, after half an hour of trying. 'We're running out of air. I think this is the end of us.'

'Yes,' Dr Trifle said. 'Funny, isn't it?'

'Funny? We're going to die down here and you think it's funny?'

'I don't mean funny ha-ha I mean funny peculiar. I just realised that I'm not afraid any more.'

'Neither am I. Maybe that's because we're running out of air. I just feel like (yawn) sleeping.'

'Me too,' Dr Trifle said. 'I think I'll just (yawn) take a nap and think things over.'

'Dr Trifle! Mrs Trifle!' Dr Squirt's voice called out. 'Can you hear me? What are you doing?'

'Oh, no!' Selby thought. 'The Trifles have given up! They've gone to sleep! I'm the only one who hasn't given up!'

Thoughts sped around and around in Selby's brain like racing cars at a speedway. He pulled the unconscious Mrs Trifle back in her seat and then hopped into her lap to take over the controls.

'We've got to be able to get out of here the same way we got in,' he thought as he pushed the controls forward and hit one wall and then another. 'But I can't find the way out because I can't see a thing! Hey, I've got it!' Selby said noticing the faint glow from the jar of Flash-

Greebies. 'If I can collect enough of them maybe I can use them as a light!'

'Dr Trifle! Mrs Trifle!' Dr Squirt's voice said. 'What are you doing?'

'Trying to get out of here, you ninny!' Selby said.

'Is–Is that you, Dr Trifle? You sound strange.'

'Well I feel strange,' Selby said, not even trying to imitate Dr Trifle's voice. 'Now leave me alone, I'm trying to concentrate.'

Selby pulled Dr Trifle's arms out of the hollow arms and put his paws in. He picked up a small flashing creature and put it in the jar. Then he went after another one and then another.

'This is too slow. At this rate it'll be hours before there's enough light to see with,' he thought. 'And we don't have hours. Already I'm getting tired and dizzy.'

Suddenly Selby saw something sparkly next to the collecting jar. Thinking that it was another Flash-Greebie he reached out and pulled it from the mud, placing it in the jar. Suddenly light burst forth from the jar lighting up the room around him.

'What was that?!' he thought. 'My goodness, it's not a creature at all. It looks like a piece broken off a chandelier or something! It's reflecting all the light from the creatures!'

Selby brought the arm with the jar in it up close to the front porthole.

'Wow! That's not a piece of glass! That's a necklace with a huge diamond in it! It's the Billion Dollar Bobble! I've found it! I'm rich! Hang on, what am I saying? I'm not anything if I can't get us out of here.'

Selby pointed the jar around the room and found the hole that the *Sea Squirt* had come in through. He turned the steering wheel and guided the submarine out into the ocean again.

'Okay,' Selby said over the radio. 'We're clear of the wreck. You can pull us up now.'

By the time the submarine reached the surface and was lifted on board the boat Selby and the Trifles were all in a deep sleep. But soon, the fresh air brought them back to life.

Author's note: So it was that Selby, once again, saved the Trifles' lives. But of course they never knew it. And this is where this story should have ended if it hadn't been for . . . well if it hadn't been for what happened next.

While the Trifles were recovering in their deck chairs, Selby wandered around with visions of riches dancing in his head. No one had noticed that Selby found the Billion Dollar Bobble but soon someone was bound to.

'We're rich! We're billionaires! Even if Dr Squirt takes half the money and leaves the Trifles with the other half, our worries are over forever. Now I can reveal my secret! I can talk to the Trifles! I won't have to work because we'll have a house full of servants,' Selby thought. 'I wish they'd hurry up and notice that the necklace is in the jar. Hmmm,' he thought as he looked over the side of the boat. 'Come to think of it, where is the jar? Did Dr Squirt take it down to his laboratory?'

Below, in a darkened room, Dr Squirt had the collecting jar and was getting ready to take the creatures out so that he could begin his studies. Slowly he tipped the contents into an aquarium and watched the tiny points of light spread around on the bottom.

'Hmmm, what's this?' he thought when the Flash-Greebies had all left the jar. 'Dr Trifle seems to have picked up a rock or something. Oh, well.'

And this is when Dr Squirt tipped the billion dollar diamond necklace out the porthole and into the sea. All of which would have been bad enough but Selby was on deck directly above the porthole and saw it go.

'The necklace!' Selby cried and, suddenly forgetting that he was the only non-swimming dog in Australia and, perhaps, the world, he dived overboard.

All of which brings us back to the beginning where Selby, half drowned, was struggling in the water. Then the dark shape began swimming around him in smaller and smaller circles.

Suddenly it came closer and nuzzled its nose in Selby's fur.

'Gulp. He's going to play with me before he eats me!' Selby squealed to himself. 'Why doesn't he just get it over with?!'

But playing, not eating, was on this creature's mind. He nuzzled Selby and then pushed him upwards. Selby broke the surface like a rocket. The splash was so loud that Dr and Mrs Trifle jumped out of their deckchairs and ran to the other side of the boat.

'It's Selby!' Mrs Trifle called. 'He's fallen in the water! Quick! Get a rowboat!'

But there was no need for rowboats. The thing that was toying with Selby wasn't really a shark, as he'd thought, but a dolphin.

'*Bleep beek squeak gleep*,' it said as it bounced Selby one more time and then hurled him up onto the deck.

'He saved your life!' Mrs Trifle said, holding Selby in her arms. 'What happened?'

'He must have fallen overboard,' Dr Trifle said. 'He's probably still too dizzy to walk.'

'*Gleep bleep squeak bleep*,' the dolphin said.

'I recognise that voice,' Selby thought as the dolphin leapt high into the air again. 'Did Dr Trifle say Dizzy? It's him! It's Dizzy the dolphin! I rescued him from Dr Squirt's research station years ago! ✌ He must have recognised me and saved me! Which just goes to show that if you do a good deed for a dolphin, he'll do a good deed for you.'

> ✌ Paw note: If you want to read another story about me, the Trifles, Dr Squirt and how I rescue a dolphin named Dizzy, read the story 'Selby Sinks to New Depths' in the book Selby's Secret.
>
> S

'Isn't that funny,' Dr Trifle said as Dizzy swam in circles around the boat balancing on his tail. 'He must be a trained dolphin.'

'I think you're right,' Mrs Trifle said. 'Look he's wearing a sparkly collar. Goodness! It's like a necklace with a huge hunk of glass hanging from it.'

'If I didn't know better,' Dr Trifle said, 'I'd say it was a diamond.'

Dr and Mrs Trifle laughed at the thought of a dolphin wearing a diamond necklace and patted Selby some more.

'And Dizzy is welcome to it,' Selby thought as Dizzy leapt again and was gone. 'Who needs all that money? I don't. I've got the best thing that anyone could ever have: Dr and Mrs Trifle. And they love me and I love them so much I could scream. Well I *could* scream but I don't think I will.'

Author's note: Well I hope you had those tissues handy. It was a happy ending but it was one of those happy endings that brought tears to my eyes when Selby told it to me. I am always touched when he tells me how much he loves the Trifles. Who needs lots of money when you have that?

FISH WISH

I wish, I wish, I wish, I wish,
That I could be a little fish
And swim around the sea and play
With other fishes night and day.

I'd dart among the seaweed and
Then rub my belly in the sand.
And when it was my time to sup
I'd gobble littler fishies up.

Hang on a minute! Don't you see?
A bigger fish might snack on me!
Forget this little fishy lark,
I think I'd rather be a shark.

Or maybe I could be a whale
And have a huge almighty tail,
More teeth than you have ever seen,
And plenty more of me between.

Of all the creatures in the sea
The biggest one's the one for me.

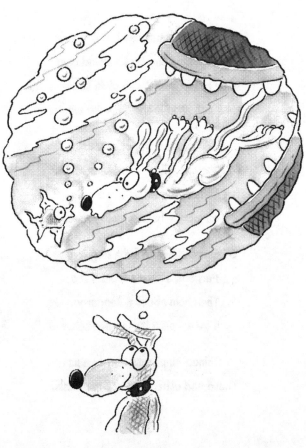

MY PET SHOP

❧

Of all the shops that I have known
There's only one that I would own.
For reasons that are plain to see
A pet shop is the shop for me.

If I could only get my wish
I'd have one filled with tanks of fish
And cuddly kittens in a heap
Then lots of birdies going cheep.

Of course there'd be a dog or two
Perhaps a panda from a zoo
Then how about a kangaroo:
A joey – with its mother too.

Rhinos, elephants and camels
These and other sorts of mammals.

Along with many many more –
Of course I'd reinforce the floor.

And then I'd let them out to play
Before I gave them all away.
When finally I'd done my dash
I'd buy another shop – for cash.

I'd play with all the pets again
And give them all away and then,
When every pet had found a home,
I'd sit and write another poem.

BowLED Out

One of these days something terrible is going to happen to me. I still shiver when I think of that trip down to the bottom of the sea. Sheeeeeesh! Soooo scary! I'm not a very **bold** dog and I **doubt** that I can stand another adventure like that.

Anyway, thanks for reading these stories. This is the seventh book. One hundred and seven (107!!) stories so far. I hope you liked them because—apart from the Trifles—you are my very favourite person.

So keep well, be good, and be happy!

Your faithful-to-the-very-end friend,

 Selby

ABOUT THE AUTHOR

Duncan Ball is an Australian author and scriptwriter, best known for his popular books for children. Among his most-loved works are the Selby books of stories plus the collections *Selby's Selection*, *Selby's Joke Book* and *Selby's Side-splitting Joke Book*. Some of these books have also been published in New Zealand, Germany, Japan and the USA, and have won countless awards, most of which were voted by the children themselves.

Among Duncan's other books are the Emily Eyefinger series about the adventures of a girl who was born with an eye on the end of her finger, and the comedy novels *Piggott Place* and

Piggotts in Peril, about the frustrations of twelve-year-old Bert Piggott forever struggling to get his family of ratbags and dreamers out of the trouble they are constantly getting themselves into.

Duncan lives in Sydney with his wife, Jill, and their cat, Jasper. Jasper often keeps Duncan company while he's writing and has been known to help by walking on the keyboard. Once, returning to his work, Duncan found the following word had mysteriously appeared on screen: ikantawq . . . .

For more information about Duncan and his books, see Selby's web site at:
www.duncanball.com.au

PIGGOTT PLACE

Duncan Ball

'Tell me what I should do with my life!' Bert wailed. 'Should I catch a boat to South America? Should I learn to play the trombone? Should I start an ostrich farm? I need your help! Give me a sign, any sign!'

Sadly, Bert was talking to the only one he trusted in the whole world: Gazza, his stuffed goat. And, once again, the goat wasn't talking …

Piggott Place is a riotous but touching comedy about twelve-year-old Bert Piggott as he struggles to keep his family of dreamers, ratbags and scoundrels together. Everyone hates the Piggotts and now the council is going to evict them from their once beautiful mansion, Piggott Place. But the authorities haven't bargained on Bert and his young friend Antigone (would-be star of stage and screen) and their crazy scheme. The question is: can two kids take on a world of adults and win?

PIGGOTTS IN PERIL

Duncan Ball

Piggotts in Peril begins with the shy and sensitive Bert Piggott accidentally finding the map to pirate treasure hidden many years ago by his great-great-great-great-grandfather. At first a quest for untold wealth seems the answer to all his problems but getting it means bringing along his scheming, ratbag family. Little does he know that what lies ahead are problems that even the pessimistic Bert could never imagine: the terror of turbulent seas aboard a 'borrowed' boat, capture by pirates, being marooned on the Isle of the Dead, and more.

Piggotts in Peril is a warm, adventure-comedy about the origins of the universe, the evolution of humankind — and pirate treasure.